Orb of Night: Lion of the West
By D.C. Bales

ISBN-13: 978-0615527864
ISBN-10: 0615527868

To my loving mom

...that is strong,

...that is wonderful,
...that is kind,

...that is smart,

...that cares,
...that is selfless,

...that loves God...
...and her children,

I dedicate this book

-D. C. Bales

Preface

When starting to write this, I already had experience with writing many other unreleased books and stories. I was greatly inspired by the eastern parts of our world when writing this book, but I have also been inspired by many other things.

Oppression is a big piece of my story; a western nation that's very powerful and very oppressive of the eastern people of our world. I decided that I would write a satire of sorts, but it is not as obvious as some pieces.

You will really have to look deep in the story to be able to see all the hidden meanings, but I will leave that up to each individual to find.

I think that people of all ages will enjoy this story in many different ways; whether someone likes satire, science-fiction or fiction of any sort they will most likely enjoy this story.

This story relates really well to things in our own world, so it should not be hard for those who know what is going on in our world to be able to find relations.

The different regions of the world are all based on real-life regions and their people are all based on real-life civilizations and cultures.

I have hope that anyone that reads this will enjoy it as much as I have enjoyed writing it.

Preview of the Storyline

Fifty-thousand years had gone by in the Eastern Region without a war. But, an oppressive nation of the Western Region launched an invasion that ended this peace.

A man named Hideaki, who was of the ancient and immortal people called the Enlightened, had stepped up to resist the western nation.

When his resistance failed to garner enough support, he found two young and faithful followers that he took along with him to find an ancient weapon: the Orb of Night.

With this ancient weapon, Hideaki could stop the western army without contest. Unfortunately, the Orb of Night was separated into nine pieces and given to nine of the different Enlightened.

Hideaki and his two followers, Volf and Skye must seek out the nine pieces and reconstruct the Orb of Night before the western nation and their disgusting and psychotic emperor, Leyb, raze the entire Eastern Region and murder all of their people.

Table of Contents

NORTHERN POLE

ENCLAVE TROVE

CENTRAL JUNGLES

WESTERN REGION

EASTERN REGION

MIDDLE ISLAND

SOUTHERN FLYING ISLANDS

Sphere Zero

PROLOGUE: Sphere Zero

The Eastern region of Sphere Zero was at peace for fifty-thousand years. There were no armies in the region for almost the entire time; not a single person of the Eastern region was prepared for the imminent firestorm of battle.

Humans on this planet can be of any color, unlike most species in the universe on other planets. Most of the racist Westerners are Orange or Red, but there are so many other colors in the world that they oppress.

Oppressive Westerners of a powerful nation came to take control of the entire Eastern region and secure the land for their leader – Leyb.

Leyb was a vile emperor; he ruthlessly destroyed and seized hundreds of other nations and tribes; he had never found anyone that could challenge his army's might until he found the Enlightened of the Eastern Region.

Enlightened were people that followed the disciplines of the oldest creatures on the planet, the Old Ones. Following these disciplines allowed the Enlightened to gain eternal life so long as they continued to practice them forever.

Armies of the Western region would soon pour out from the hills and the Eastern region was to fall beneath their might if the Enlightened did not use their power to stop them; unfortunately, choosing a side in a battle would strip an Enlightened of their immortality.

Therefore, every Enlightened Easterner must make the choice between immortality and saving their entire region.

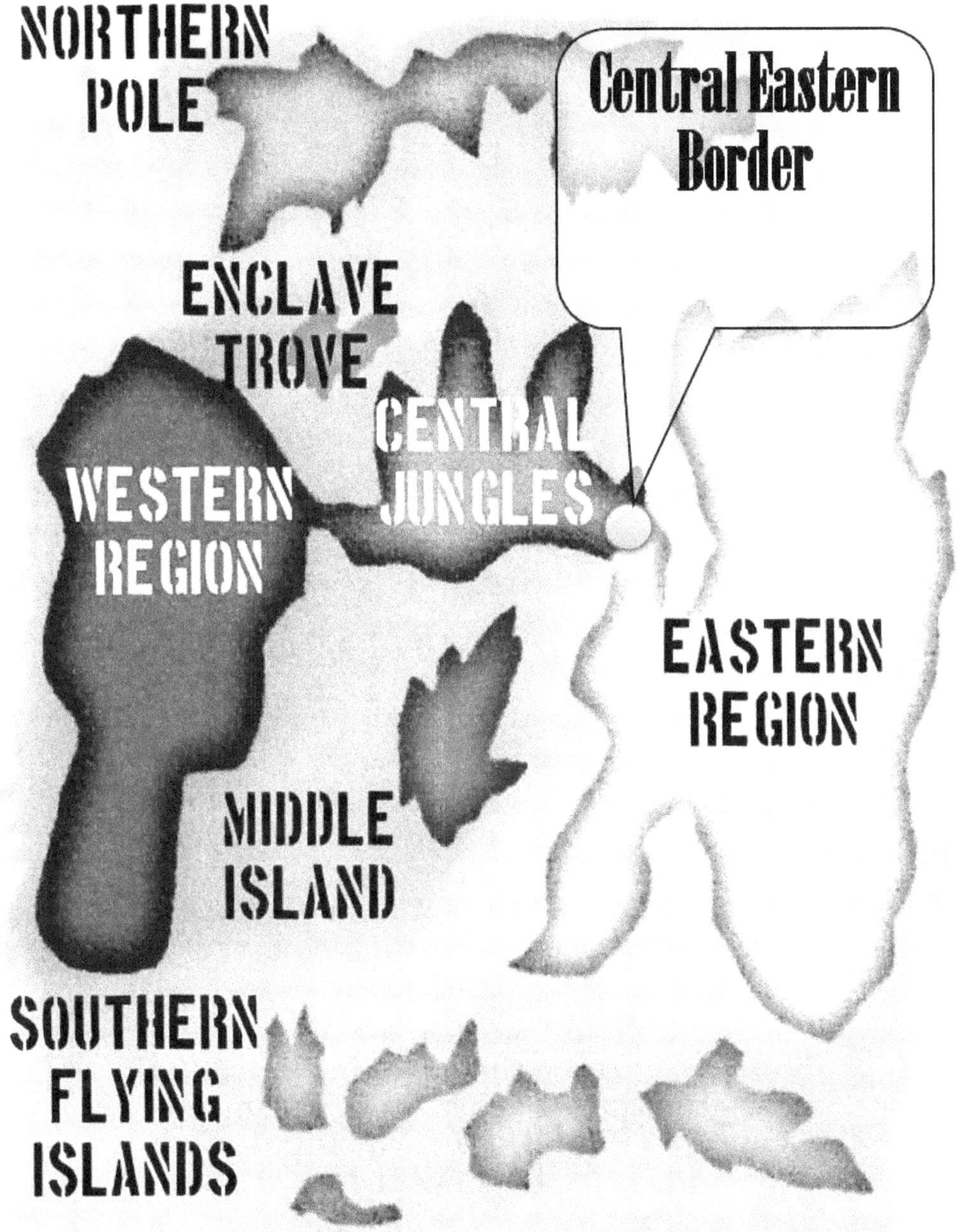
NORTHERN POLE
Central Eastern Border
ENCLAVE TROVE
CENTRAL JUNGLES
WESTERN REGION
EASTERN REGION
MIDDLE ISLAND
SOUTHERN FLYING ISLANDS

Sphere Zero

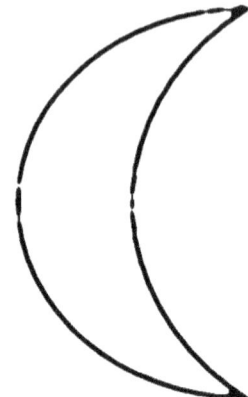

Chapter I: Lion of the West

Leyb was considered to be a merciless, wicked and disgusting man; he enjoyed invading nations for the simple pleasure he got in killing and in seeing the destruction and chaos he caused.

He would sometimes invade a nation, encircling it and declaring anarchy within its borders; at these times he would watch the nation tear itself apart from within and once the people were withered to almost nothing he would enter it and kill whoever was left.

He was known throughout most of the world, except for the Eastern region which had few people concerned with things of war or violence in other parts of the world.

Disgusting as it sounds, this man once sacrificed his own son to defeat another nation; he doesn't care about his own family – his daughter, his previous wives or his dead son.

Westerners fear him and hate him, but they follow him because they have no other choice. None of the Westerners want the wars, but Leyb is simply too powerful for the voice of the people to change whatsoever.

This terrible emperor was called the Lion of the West by a man of the Eastern region; this man, Hideaki, was an Enlightened. He simply wanted to warn the people of the army that was headed to their region to kill and destroy, but the people were too preoccupied with their peaceful lives to care what was about to happen.

Being an Enlightened, Hideaki knew that it was his responsibility to gain the trust of the people and rally forces against Leyb; he knew that waiting for him to arrive in their region was simply suicide.

Hideaki traveled across the entire Eastern region in search of groups that would help him defend, but he found very few; the people he found helped him build a large hideout where he would gather his forces and construct defenses as needed.

Organizing their attacks and strategies for the coming war would be done in this new fortress, hidden underground. He had a few hundred on his side ready to fight, but they were nothing compared to the five-thousand man army of Leyb marching toward the Eastern region.

Leyb may be a disgusting man, but he at least pretends to care about his daughter, Anastasia.

Anastasia was supposedly ignorant of what her father had done in the world; she was said to believe that the army is simply just her personal guard and that they are going on a long vacation as usual.

She is fourteen years old and yet unlearned in the ways of war and fighting. Her father wants her to be a weakling in case she ever wishes to rebel against him, but he does not wish to kill her because he does have a small amount of love for her left.

"Daddy," said Anastasia, "where are we going to visit on this vacation?"

"We're visiting the Eastern region, dear." Leyb said to her, "The people there also want to give me control of everything; just like all of the other people in the world."

"Oh." She said simply, "That's probably just because you're the best emperor in the world! And the best daddy, too!"

"I am the best at everything, Annie."

"I told you to stop calling me that... I like my full name."

"Alright, Anastasia." He said, "Well... I have to go to meet my council; we need to discuss our invasion... I mean our persuasions of the Eastern nations."

"Okay, daddy; I love you!"

"Love you too, Annie... Ehm, I mean Anastasia." He said with a smile.

Leyb walked out from Anastasia's carriage and to the carriage of his highest generals; these are some of the most fearsome and despicable people in the world.

Generals serving under Leyb were gathered from many corners of the world. When Leyb invaded a nation he would visit the prisons and find the most evil and wicked of criminals that have experience being leaders of different sorts.

Assigning them generals of armies and telling them to have fun by slaughtering and destroying in the world was the most likely thing for him to do with dangerous criminals, rather than kill them and 'waste their valuable blood,' as he always said.

Five generals were all that were left at this point; most of the generals he had hired in the past were killed in battle, had killed themselves, had been killed in their sleep, had betrayed Leyb and executed, had ran off or had simply disappeared.

First, one of the generals still serving was a mass-murderer; Nazar was his name. His kills number in the millions, which was strangely more than Leyb himself. The emperor was impressed by this man's ways and took him as one of his generals; Leyb told him that he was allowed to kill anyone he wanted with his armies.

Second, there was a man who murdered only three people but he murdered them in torturous and disgusting ways that caused the most terrible of pain. His name was Ornias. One time he carved the skin off of a young boy slowly over the course of five days until the boy finally died. The next murder he kidnapped an elderly woman and strapped her about a couple of meters above a fire and allowed the heat to slowly melt her and burn her over the course of a week. The final murder was of his mother; he tied her to a wall and each day he would take a limb from her body. Her right arm, her left arm, her right leg, her left leg and finally he beheaded her.

Third, a female general who was known throughout the Central Jungles; she was thought to be a monster or evil goddess that stalked children and killed them when they were alone. Her name was Usha, which was pronounced Oosh-Uh. Unlike the other generals, Usha found Leyb and wanted to kill his daughter, but he instead asked her if she wanted some armies to command and she accepted this offer and continued to kill children, but with the help of an entire army to bring children to her to murder every day.

Fourth and fifth, two generals that were once partners in crime, husband and wife. Their names were Ayé and Kione. They robbed seven entire nations of all of their stores of gold by becoming high ranking leaders within; they then declared anarchy and watched as the people killed one another. These two are the ones that inspired Leyb to do the same thing to many other nations in the future after they joined him.

"Anastasia still doesn't suspect anything, does she?" Usha asked.

"I don't think so," Leyb responded, "she just doesn't know anything about war or violence and she still thinks I'm the perfect father."

The group of generals had a great laugh at the idea of Leyb being the perfect father.

"So, what is our battle plan?" asked Leyb, "Are we going to surround each city and declare anarchy?"

"No." Ayé responded, "We have decided that because of this being the last region on the main continent, we're going to have the last bit of fun we can with the region. We're all going to do the individual cities differently. Each of us will take one-thousand of the five-thousand soldiers that we have brought with us and we will all cause chaos in the region in whatever way we see fit."

"I like this plan," Leyb said, "it sounds very fun for you five. However, what am I supposed to do while you five have your fun?"

"Good point..." Ayé said, "Why don't my husband and I take only one-thousand of the soldiers together and you can take the final one-thousand soldiers. This way it will be fair for everyone."

"Perfect plan!" Leyb announced, "How long until we arrive and are able to start?"

"It will be less than a week, but we're not sure exactly how long because we don't have maps of everything along the way." said Usha."

Back in Anastasia's tent, Anastasia was talking to her personal guard – a woman named Evesmerelda; it is pronounced E-Vesmerelda.

Evesmerelda is a strong woman that is highly trusted by Anastasia, but not by her father; Leyb suspects that Evesmerelda may someday betray him but he has kept her in his service to keep Anastasia protected and uninformed of the wars. If she were to disappear then Anastasia would have asked questions as to what happened to her.

Leyb hired Evesmerelda in the same way that he hired his generals – at a prison in a country that he was invading. Evesmerelda was in prison for the kidnapping, torturing and murdering of hundreds of men. She was once a campaigner for women's rights in her country, but she went too far and began to murder in vengeance when she knew that never in her lifetime would Evesmerelda see the rights she and all other women in her country deserved.

Fortunately, her time in prison allowed her to rethink her life and her goals and when Leyb hired her he asked her to become a general; however, while he was asking her to join him his daughter, Anastasia was attacked by Usha – which led to Usha being hired by Leyb.

Jumping to the rescue wasn't Leyb but Evesmerelda; Anastasia was only four at this time and she has told her father and Evesmerelda that she doesn't remember being attacked or anything about that time other than meeting her personal guard and best friend, Evesmerelda.

"Dad doesn't know anything yet, does he?" Anastasia asked.

"No," Evesmerelda responded, "he still thinks that you're a helpless and ignorant little girl. He just can't help but not realize it, though; he never talks to you for more than a few minutes and he never really asks questions that allow him to get to know you."

"So will our plan for the country work, Evesmerelda?"

"Yeah, I think so. Let's not talk more about the plan until your dad's invasion begins, though. I just don't think it's safe to be talking about betraying and killing your father right in the middle of his army caravan..."

"Good point." Anastasia said with a grin.

Leyb's army marched ever closer to the Eastern region; the Central Jungles were all under his control and nothing was on his path to slow him down.

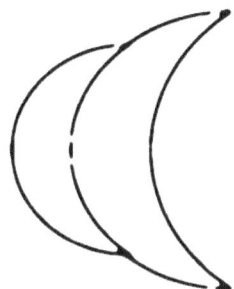

Chapter II: Fleeting Serenity

Ignorant of the invasion just around the corner, the people of the Eastern region continued their peaceful everyday lives.

Hideaki, the Enlightened man leading the resistance has come to the main town where the invasion from the West and the defense against it will begin. His secret base was hidden in the cliffs to the Southeast of the city.

In the peaceful town, a young teenage girl by the name of Skye was walking through a local market, unaware of the soldiers surrounding the town.

She was seventeen years old, dark pink-skinned, about one and a half meters tall and has a long braided bunch of hair going down her back with red bows dotting it all over in seemingly random places.

The most interesting feature of Skye was her tattoo on her forehead; a heart on top of a cross or star of sorts.

People would stare at this tattoo as she passed them by and they would wonder what the tattoo represented.

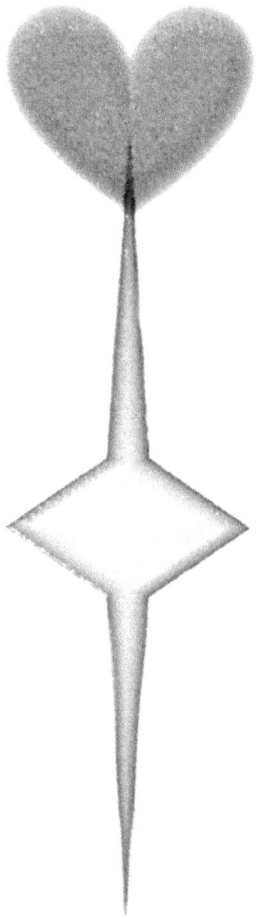

"Can I get an orange for free?" she asked a seller, "I have no food or money."

"No money, no food." he responded, "You think I'm stupid?"

"But I have nothing... my family excommunicated me and I have no one and nowhere to go. Please, can I have at least something to eat?!"

"No! Now get out of here, you bum!"

"Okay..." she said with tears running down her face. Skye then walked away slowly, thinking of herself as worthless.

Skye was then walking through the local market all alone when the attack on the city finally began. An explosion shook the entire city and a nearby pillar became unbalanced; it began to fall and Skye was too distracted by her broken heart to realize that it was about to land on top of her.

Just as she was about to be crushed a green colored teenage boy pushed her out of the immediate danger of the collapsing column.

"What are you doing?!" she cried as she slapped him in the face.

"I was saving your life!" he said, "That pillar almost killed you!"

"Oh my... What happened here?!"

"Seriously? You didn't see it?"

"See what?"

"A giant explosion just caused the entire city to start shaking."

"Where?!"

"Wow. You're really out of it; the explosion happened right next to you! Are you doing alright? I think that explosion might have hurt you more than it looked like..."

"No... I'm just... depressed."

"Depressed? That doesn't make you stupid! You should have at least seen the explosion!"

"Stupid?! You're the stupid idiot that pushed me to the ground!"

"To save you!"

"Whatever... What's going on? What made the explosion?"

"I don't know... Well, what's your name, anyway?"

"Skye..."

"That's a pretty name. My name's Volf, thanks for asking..."

"Sorry... My mind's just going all over the place right now, Volf. I do like your name, though; I've never heard it before."

"Thanks, Skye. Yeah, we really should get out of this marketplace; it looks like the entire thing is going to collapse on top of us and that ceiling looks heavy..."

"Yeah, let's go..."

"Something wrong?"

"No, it's just... why are you helping me? I'm just a worthless throwaway daughter... my parents disowned me and my family completely excommunicated me. Why would a random person like you care about me?"

"Showing love to everyone in the world is a good thing, I think. Don't you?"

"Yes, but I've... just not met anyone else willing to help me until I've met you. Everyone else here in the market just wants money and couldn't care less if I live or die."

"Those sellers probably just thought you were a thief; it's understandable. You should ask for help from regular people not the marketplace sellers."

"Yeah... Anyway, let's get out of here before it collapses."

Volf and Skye ran out of the marketplace together only to see their city burning and people screaming and being killed; they could not hear the screams from within the noisy and crumbling market, but now they see what caused the explosion within.

"Crap." Volf said.

"Yeah... that."

"Come on!" said a man, "We're going through the sewers to escape the city!"

The two of them decided to follow the man into the sewers, which were also crumbling in the attack. Screams of women, children and even men could be heard coming from the streets above.

"Where are we going?" Volf asked.

"We're going to the cliffs to the southeast of the city." the man said, "There is a secret base hidden in the cliffs where we can hide."

"A secret base?" Skye asked.

"Yes, it was built in anticipation of this attack. We also tried to warn the town, but the government would not listen to us and stopped us from forming any defenses in the city itself. They also stopped us from warning many people."

Eventually, they reached edge of town and the sewer exit. Outside of the sewer was a group of soldiers; these evil soldiers were killing everyone that tried to escape.

"Oh no..." the man said, "We need to turn around and go... back."

"They followed us!" a woman screamed, "We're all going to die!"

"We have to fight them!" Volf shouted, "We have no other choice!"

"I agree!" the man leading them said, "Attack!"

Volf and the man rushed toward the exit and attacked the soldiers. Volf was nearly stabbed by a spear but he was able to dodge it and pull a knife out to stab the soldier himself.

The man wasn't so lucky; he was impaled through the belly and left on the ground to die.

"No!" Skye cried, "You disgusting people stabbed that poor man!"

Skye's strange tattoo began to glow and she began to scream; the heart on the tattoo glowed red and the star glowed blue. It came forth from her head and formed a staff of sorts.

"Burn in my cosmic energy..." she muttered as she pointed her staff at the soldiers blocking the exit.

"Universal…" she yelled as most nearby light was sucked into the heart of the staff, "Complete…" she said as a black ring appeared around the heart, "Annihilation!"

A black sandstorm appeared around the staff and rushed at the soldiers, disintegrating them into ashes.

The light in the surrounding area returned to normal and the staff appeared back into her forehead.

The soldiers that were following them through the sewers from the city then turned and ran back after seeing their comrades be turned to nothing by a young girl.

"Wow!" Volf exclaimed, "What just happened, Skye?!"

"Now you hate me too… See! That's why my family excommunicated me! It's not my fault. I didn't ask for that power!"

"No, no… It's just fine, Skye!" the dying man exclaimed on the ground, "You saved all of these people around you! Now, go! You must find a man named Hideaki. He will help you… and you can help… him."

The dying man took his last breath and finally passed away; Skye closed his eyes for him.

"We should bury him before we go, Volf."

"But we don't have enough time." he responded, "We have to go, now, before the soldiers come back with more people."

"Okay..." she said as they walked out of the sewer and into the fields below the cliffs.

"So, Skye," Volf said, "what did you do to those soldiers, anyway? Like, what was that power?"

"I can't tell you... Maybe someday you'll know, but I really can't tell you. My tattoo won't allow me to tell you..."

"Won't allow you to tell me?"

"Yeah... I just can't say anymore than that, I'm sorry. Let's just pretend it never happened and get out of here."

"Okay... I'm still going to keep asking you about it, though."

"I'm going to still not saying anything about it, though."

"Fine, fine." Volf said, "So, we need to find that Hideous guy or whatever the man said."

"He said Hideaki, you idiot!"

"Oh, right..."

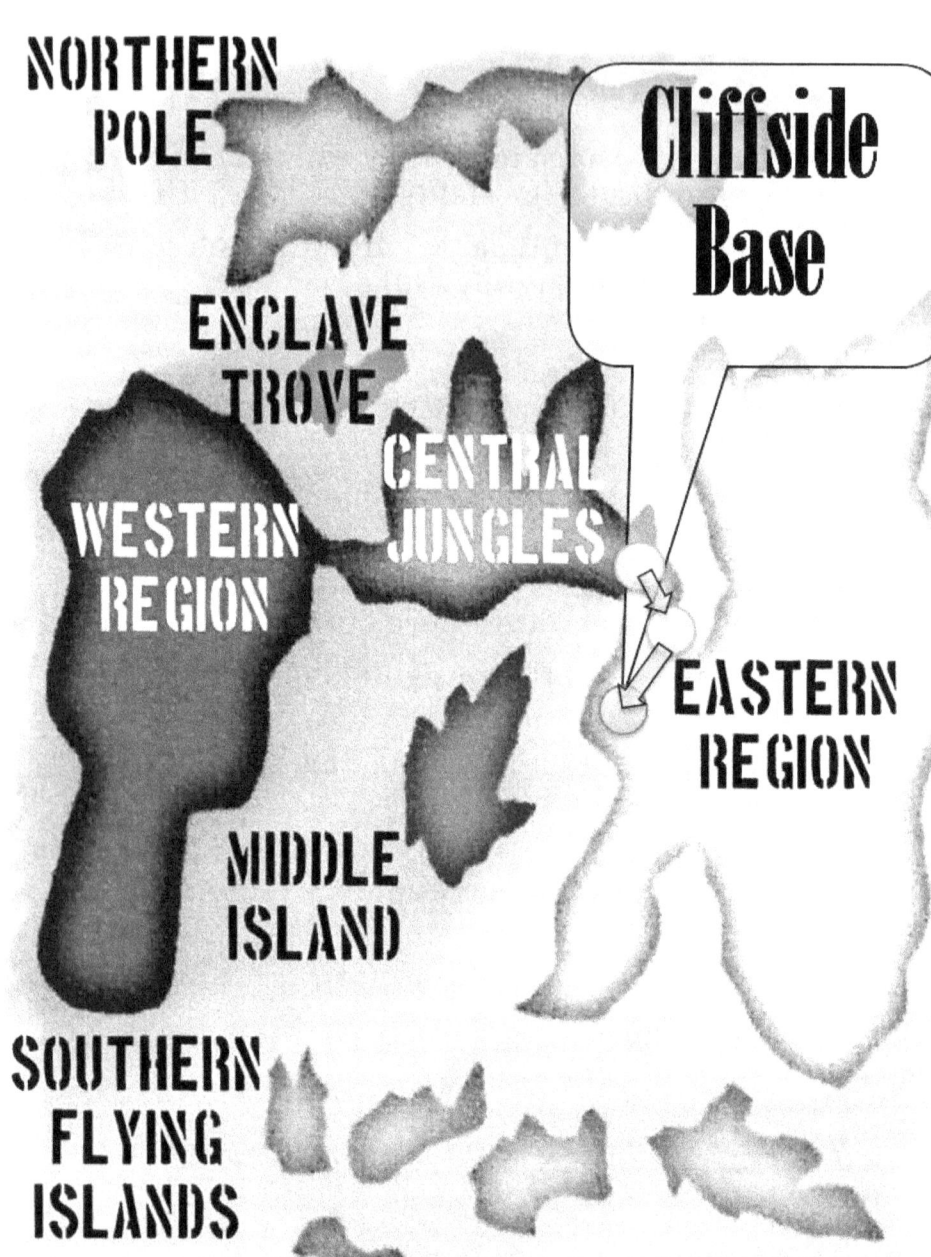

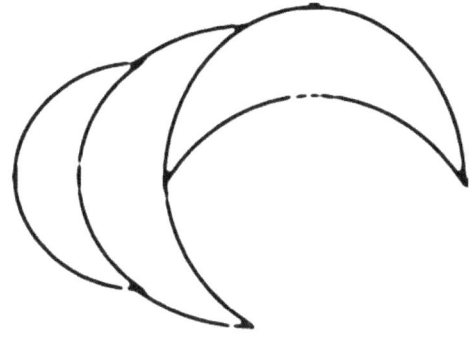

Chapter III: Crescent of the Cliffside

After wandering the Cliffside for hours Volf, Skye and the others following them were ready to set up a camp because nighttime was beginning to fall on the land; the sun was still visible, but barely.

Their city could clearly be seen at a short distance from their location. It was burning and screams could still be heard coming from within its boundaries.

"How could there still be people left alive?" Volf asked.

"Those disgusting men are probably having fun torturing people; they aren't here to take our city, they're just here to have fun killing everyone..."

"Hell yeah, we are!" said a voice from behind some nearby trees, "And we're going to have some fun with you guys next."

"Soldiers!" a woman yelled, "We're all going to die!"

"Skye," Volf said, "can you use that power again and get rid of them?"

"I... no, I don't control the power. It comes out only when there's no other way for me to survive; which means there are other ways for us to survive here..."

"How?!" Volf asked.

"I don't know, idiot! Can't you do something?! You tried to fight the soldiers last time. Maybe you can beat them all up?"

"What the hell is wrong with you?" Volf asked, "I was just being an idiot when I attacked them last time... There are like twenty of them now!"

The soldiers then began killing everyone. Each of the evil men had their own ways of killing the people and their own weapons.

Some used a bow and arrows, some used knives, some used swords, spears and other stabbing weapons and some even chose to beat the poor people to death with their bare hands.

Finally, the soldiers rushed at Volf and Skye; Volf dodged one and punched the man on the back of his neck, cutting off his brain from his spine and therefore paralyzing him.

The other soldiers were then more careful; they all surrounded him.

"I guess that's it for me." Volf said with his eyes closed and tears beginning to fall from his eyes.

"I'll take him!" One soldier exclaimed as he slowly walked toward Volf; this soldier carried a small knife as his weapon of choice.

Volf then opened his eyes and saw the man walking toward him; he took a fighting stance but as he did another soldier hit him with a bullwhip which struck him on the right cheek and gave him a huge cut.

Volf reached for his face, trying to mend the painful cut as the soldier with the knife jumped at him. Volf dodged the knife but the soldiers just kept swinging it at him.

"Come onnn, guyyy!" said a drunk soldier, "That kid keeps dodgin' yer' swings! Let me kill 'im!"

After dodging the knife for around five minutes, the other soldiers grew restless and angry that the soldier was failing to even hit Volf once.

"That's it!" said a female soldier, "You're such a weakling!"

She jumped at the soldier who kept missing his stabs at Volf and snapped the soldier's neck.

"General Usha!" the drunk soldier exclaimed, "What are ya' doin?!"

"Teaching you all a lesson." She said, "If you fail to follow my orders then you're useless. I'll take this kid myself."

"Who the hell are you?"

"Didn't you hear? I'm General Usha."

"Yeah... I still don't know who you are..."

"Alright, so you want more than a name. I'm the most powerful person on this planet; I could kill anyone and survive anything."

"Well... why did you kill your own soldier?"

"He was useless."

"So you kill him?! You're a terrible woman!"

"All of Leyb's generals are terrible." She responded as she pulled a bullwhip from her back, "You remember that whipping on your face from a few moments ago, right?"

"So you're the one that did that!" Volf said.

"No. I just killed the soldier that did it, because he was useless, too."

"Wow. I can't believe you! You're just a disgusting monster!"

"Now you're getting it." Usha said as she snapped her whip in the air, "I'm going to have some fun killing you."

Usha then whipped Volf on his right arm and he screamed in pain.

"Oh my Old Ones, this is so fun!" She said as she whipped Volf again on his right arm.

"Please stop!" Volf said with tears gushing down his face, "It hurts so much! Please!"

"Nah, this is fun." She said as she whipped him once more, this time on his left leg.

Volf fell to the ground, bleeding from multiple areas on his body.

"Please stop... Please." He begged.

"Old Ones!" she exclaimed, "This is so awesome!"

She then repeatedly whipped him as he cried and begged for help and for it to stop. Skye just watched in horror as it all happened.

It looked as if Volf was about to die; he began to cough up blood and most of his body looked like a disfigured corpse. He was drowning in his own blood.

"This is the best day ever!" Usha exclaimed with great enjoyment. "Unfortunately, I think it's time to end this. I had fun torturing you though, kid."

Usha had set her bullwhip down to watch Volf in his agony.

She reached to pick it up and as she did her soldiers were consumed in dust like when Skye used her strange Universal Complete

Annihilation attack, yet the dust was only a normal brownish color.

"What the hell happened?!" Usha exclaimed, "My soldiers were cut to pieces!"

Every soldier with her had been minced into bits on the ground and none had survived; Usha then looked to Skye, remembering what her scouts had told her about a young girl with a magical tattoo on her forehead.

"You!" Usha said, "I killed my scouts because I thought they were lying, but you are real! You killed half of my scouts and now you killed some of my soldiers!"

"It wasn't me! I did kill the scouts but I didn't do it on purpose... I didn't kill the soldiers, though... I..."

"Shut up!" Usha commanded, "You stupid little tramp!"

Usha rushed at Skye and as she did a strange voice came from the trees.

"Wrong person, General Usha." A man's voice said.

"Who's that?!"

"I am Hideaki."

"I heard about you." Usha claimed, "You're the leader of that pointless resistance. Too bad that telling me about you didn't save those people's lives in the town."

"You vile creature!" said Hideaki, "You will die!"

"I can't die."

"Universal Chaos!" Hideaki screamed as his beard twirled in circles and a tornado came forth from it.

Literally sharp winds pushed Usha back into a large tree behind her; she tried to stand her ground but the winds began chopping her into pieces until she was nothing but goop on the ground.

"Oh my Old Ones!" Skye exclaimed as she covered her eyes in horror of the terrible sight in front of her.

Soldiers were disgusting piles of meat and Usha herself was, too. Seeing a person who was just alive and well – that she just had a conversation with – be minced to pieces right in front her was too much to bear the sight of.

Hideaki then ran to Volf and kneeled down over him; Hideaki was a brightly yellow colored man, with a very long beard and no hair on his very shiny and probably waxed head.

"Body Undoing!" Hideaki said and green light seeped from his body and encroached over Volf, healing his body, but leaving scars all about.

"Thank you." Volf said as he fell asleep almost instantly.

Hideaki simply smiled and picked him up.

"How did you do that?!" Skye asked.

"Being an Enlightened gives you powers that the Old Ones had." He responded, "If you followed the ways of the Old Ones then you too would gain your own powers."

"So... you're Enlightened?"

"Yes, dear." He responded, "I guess you've never seen another Enlightened, before?"

"No, I have... that's why I was surprised to see that you are. My dad is Enlightened."

"Ah. I know who you are, then. You are Skye, the girl with the mystical tattoo."

"I knew you'd hate me just like my dad... I'll just go away by myself."

"No!" he cried, "I mean no disrespect. Your father is a terrible man for banishing you for having powers you cannot control. He should have taught you how to control it with the power of Enlightenment rather than force you to leave."

"It can be controlled?!"

"Yes, dear. Come with me into my hidden base and I will explain everything that I can."

Hideaki led Skye and the rest of the people left in the area around many of the cliffs, between trees and through caverns. Finally, they reached a cavern hidden at the top of the cliffs.

"This is the entrance." Hideaki said, "I'll bring you two and the rest of the people to a place where you can rest for the day. Volf and you are both important to me and I need to talk to you both as soon as Volf wakes up."

Hideaki gave them a place to sleep and the next morning Volf woke up after Skye had sat next to him the whole night.

"Skye?"

"Yeah, it's me Volf."

"How long have you been sitting there?"

"Most of the night..." she responded, "I just thought I would lose you..."

"Skye, we just met not that long ago. I don't think you would be that sad if I died."

"I know. Most people don't get attached that quickly. I just don't have anyone, so I get attached really easily..."

"Oh. Well, that's fine, I understand. Thanks for being there for me, Skye."

"Yeah..." Skye said with her cheeks turning red. Hideaki then walked into the room.

"Volf, you're awake!" he said.

"Yeah, thanks for helping me, Mr. Hideous."

"It's Hideaki!"

"Idiot!" Skye said.

"Oh right... sorry."

"Anyway," Hideaki continued, "Come with me, you two. I have to teach you two much in a very short time."

Hideaki then taught Skye and Volf over the course of the next two weeks how to control some of the powers of the Enlightened.

Skye had trouble controlling the powers of her tattoo, but she gained some ability to control it. Volf gained only one power and that is the power that Hideaki used to defeat Usha and her soldiers.

"Universal Chaos!" Volf screamed as a tornado shot from his spinning hands; the tornado barely cut the target dummy, but it could still push it back quite a ways.

"It's still not as powerful as yours..." Volf said.

"Yes, but you will grow in power over time. You need to continue down the path of Enlightenment in the future when we find peace again. Then, you can gain immortality and far greater power."

"So are we done training now, then?" Skye asked.

"Yes, we need to stop Leyb soon." Hideaki said, "He has already taken over one-fourth of the Eastern region and his influence will only continue to spread until he rules everything."

"How can we stop him, Hideaki?" Skye asked. "I would be able to stop him if I could control the tattoo's most powerful attack..."

"Yes, the Universal Complete Annihilation attack." Hideaki said, "It is the most powerful collection of cosmic energy anywhere."

"So you've heard of it, before?!" Skye asked.

"Yes. The only other person able to use that power is the Ruler of Death, Cizin."

"The ruler of death…"

"Yes. You have the power of the Ruler of Death within you; I'm not quite sure how you got it, but you should avoid using it at all costs."

"Is it really that dangerous?"

"It is more dangerous than anything else in the universe. If your beam misses its target then the target will still be destroyed, but so will the entire universe! Only use the power as a last resort and make sure you hit the target if you do!"

"Oh my Old Ones…" Skye said, "I have the power to destroy everything?!"

"Yes, but don't worry about it. I've taught you how to avoid being taken over by the tattoo. Just follow the ways of the Old Ones and you will defeat any power that tattoo has over you."

"So, if we can't use that power then what can we use?" Skye asked.

"The Orb of Night."

"The what?" Volf asked.

"We Enlightened forged it to keep peace in our world forever, but it ended up being far too powerful to allow existence, so we split it into nine crescent-shaped pieces and hid them."

"Alright, let's go get them then!" Skye said.

"Well... Each Enlightened only knows about one of them. I hold one here in my hand and eight other Enlightened know the locations of the rest."

"So we have to find the other Enlightened?" Volf asked.

"Yes."

"That's why you trained us!" Volf exclaimed, "You needed only a small team of magical fighters to help you locate the Orb of Night. That way you won't even need an army!

"Exactly!"

"So are we leaving now?"

"We are leaving tomorrow morning. Get some sleep and pack lightly; we need only our most essential supplies."

The next morning they set off on their adventure; Hideaki, Skye and Volf knew the road ahead was dangerous but they were ready and they had packed lightly.

"Skye," Volf said, "why is half your backpack filled with red bows?"

"Hideaki said to pack the essentials!"

"I don't think I understand the word essential very well..." Hideaki said.

"Shut up! I need my red bows... or I like them, anyway."

"Okay," Volf said, "Whatever you say..."

"Skye," Hideaki said, "does your liking of bows have anything to do with that tattoo?"

"No!" she exclaimed, "Well... maybe. I didn't like them until a little bit after the tattoo... Never mind, let's keep going."

"What's wrong, Skye?" Volf asked.

"Nothing, idiot! Just keep going!"

"Fine, fine..." Volf said with a grin on his face.

"What are you smiling at?!" Skye asked.

"Nothing. I'm not smiling..."

"Whatever, idiot..."

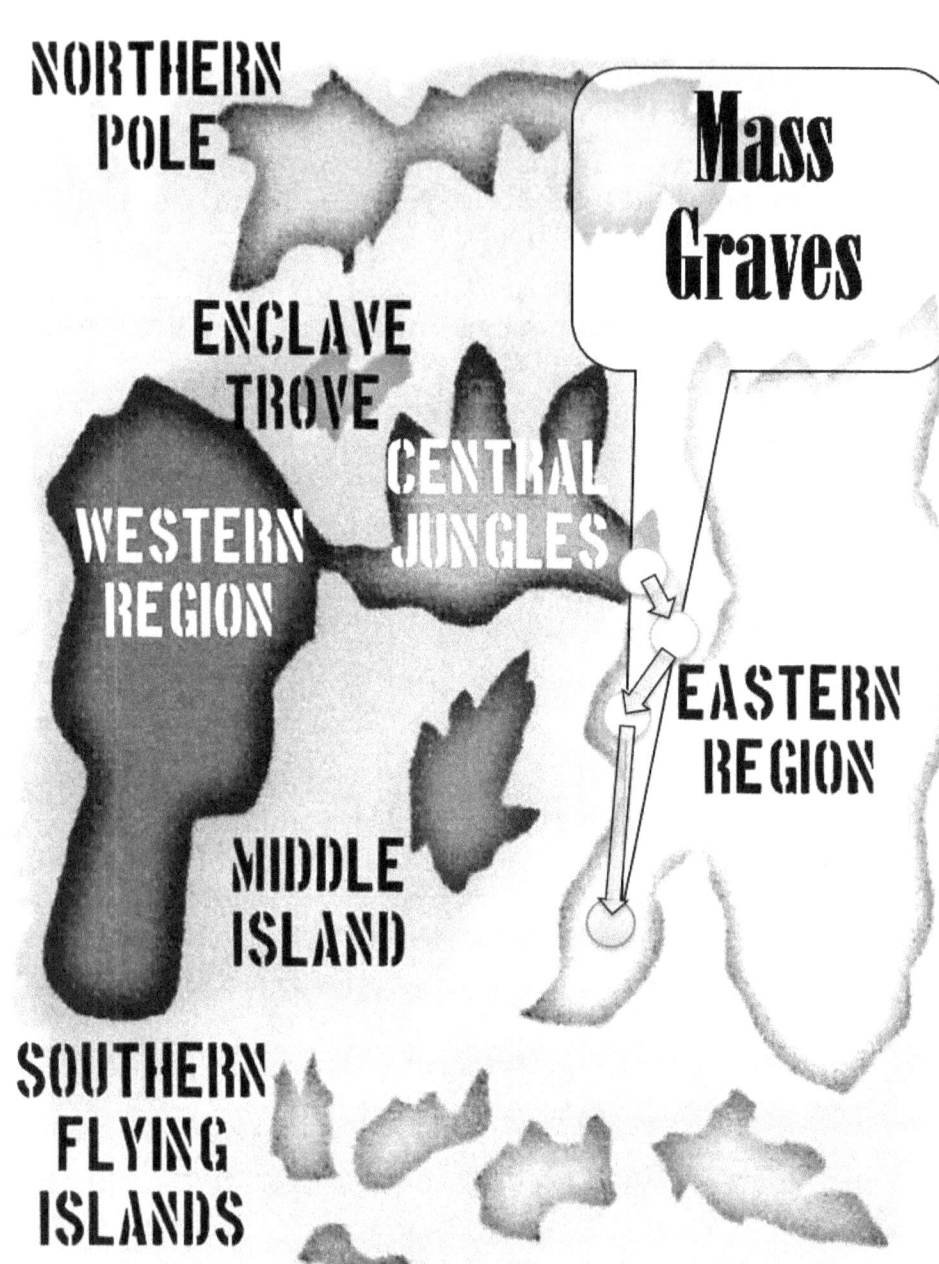

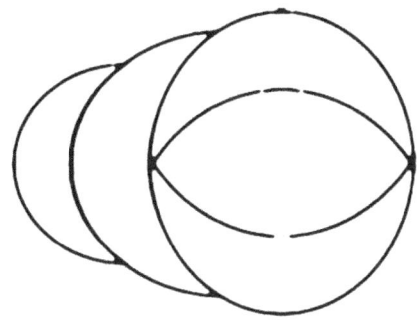

Chapter IV: Mass Graves

Traveling for seven days led them to the former home of one of the Enlightened men; the town seems to have already been destroyed by Leyb's army. Everyone they could see was dead.

"No..." Hideaki said, "We have to go to my old friend's home immediately! He lives in the temple of Old Ones at the top of these hills."

"How did Leyb's army already get this far?!" Skye asked.

"Leyb probably split his forces to invade in separate directions." Volf said.

"Remember," said Hideaki, "we spent two weeks training and a week traveling here, so they've had plenty of time to take most of the Eastern region already – if they have split their forces."

"Anyway," Volf interrupted, "which way to your friend's house?"

"Well, this place looks very different now... filled with dead bodies, burnt down buildings, crumbling ground and many other things... Let's just walk up the hill until we can see his house... if it's still there."

There were huge graves in the area; graves filled with thousands of bodies in each one. Corpses were all just piled up in a chaotic fashion.

"Are they going to do anything about these bodies?" Skye asked.

"Normally a person would, yes." Hideaki said, "However, Leyb and his armies are far from normal. They are vile and evil people."

Hideaki led them through hundreds of piles of bodies, with each pile holding thousands of dead bodies. There were even dead animals piled in with the dead humans.

"Ew!" Skye shrieked, "They killed everything! I see a chicken, a dog, a cat... Oh my Old Ones..."

"Like I said, they're evil. Don't be surprised if we see something worse in the town ahead. We're just on the outskirts of the town, so far..."

"Hideaki," Volf said, "Do you think your friend is still alive? It looks like everyone is probably dead..."

"Maybe. Enlightened are hard to kill; if an Enlightened follows the ways of the Old

Ones without wavering whatsoever, then that Enlightened cannot be killed. Unfortunately, even the slightest mishap can take away our immortality."

"So, are you immortal, Hideaki?" Volf asked.

"No. Not anymore. I gave up my immortality to fight Leyb's armies and save people who do not follow the ways of the Old Ones. Sadly, Enlightenment doesn't allow us to choose sides, therefore I lost my immortality."

"Are you going to become immortal again when the war is over, Hideaki?" Skye asked.

"I can't." he said, "Once an Enlightened gives up immortality it is gone forever."

"Wow!" Skye said, "You gave up your life for us, then!"

"Yes... Everything I had is gone, but it is worth it to save everyone in our region!"

"Hideous," Volf said, "You rule."

"It's Hideaki!" he screamed.

"Right, sorry! Hideaki!" Volf quickly said.

Finally at the top of the hill in the town, the three of them could see the top of Hideaki's friend's house.

"There it is." Hideaki said, "But wait... there's something else up ahead. Let's hide behind those bushes over there!"

Hiding behind some nearby bushes, the group encroached upon the mansion-sized house and saw that it was surrounded.

"Who are those people?" Skye asked.

"That's one of Leyb's generals." Hideaki responded, "Nazar. He's a man who has killed millions of people... by himself."

"By himself?" Volf asked.

"Yes. I haven't seen him with my own eyes, but I've heard about him. He has strange powers that allow him to force an individual's own body to kill itself. He only needs to touch you to make it happen; stay away from him and you will be fine..."

"Hey!" a voice screamed, "Who's hiding in those bushes?!"

"We've been spotted!" Hideaki said, "Run!"

The three of them turned tails and ran but they ran straight into an ambush of hundreds of soldiers. Nowhere could they see a place to run – they were caught.

"So," Nazar said while walking around a nearby corner, "You thought you would pay the man inside a visit? Maybe he will open his doors for you, then."

"Ah, I see that you can't get into his dojo." Hideaki said, "He is an Enlightened and cannot be killed."

"Then why does he not come out and simply kill us all?" Nazar asked.

"That's because choosing sides will take his immortality away." Volf said.

"Idiot!" Skye said, "You shouldn't have told them that!"

"Too late." Nazar said, "We've already killed everyone else in the town because this man would not open the door for any of them, but now it's time to try you three. Maybe he'll know one of you."

Nazar had his soldiers drag the three of them to the man's door. He then proceeded to knock on the door of the dojo.

"Are you home?" Nazar asked, "If so, you'd better open up now. I have…"

Nazar then turned around and looked to the three of them.

"What are your names?" he asked, almost as if he was embarrassed for not having asked already.

"Hideaki is my name. The boy is Volf and the girl is Skye."

"Very well." Nazar said, proceeded with an almost sincere "Thank you."

Nazar then turned back to the door and knocked once again.

"I have a girl named Skye, a boy named Volf and a man here by the name of –"

"Go away." the man inside said, "I don't know these people in this town!"

"These people aren't from this town." Nazar said, "Now let me finish their names.

The last one is an old man by the name of Hideaki."

"Hideaki..." the man inside repeated, "The door is now unlocked... But only for him."

"Thank you, sir." Nazar said as he turned back to the group.

Hideaki stared at Nazar with an angry gaze. He almost seemed to fear Hideaki because of it.

"So, little old man." Nazar said, "You're going to go inside, alone. Then, if you kill the man inside before ten minutes is gone, I won't kill these two young friends of yours."

"What?!" Hideaki said, "Leave them be! They have nothing to do with any of this!"

"You're right." Nazar said, "I'll just kill them now!"

Nazar then rushed at Volf, picked him up by his shirt and reached to touch him on his chest; just as he was about to touch Volf, the dojo's front side exploded and five spheres of fire came forth from it.

Four of the fireballs hit the areas around the group and the ensuing infernos consumed all of the Nazar's company of one-thousand soldiers, along with most of the city.

The fifth came down to strike at Nazar himself; Nazar then put his finger tips together and held his hands as if he were holding a ball.

A sphere of ice formed in his hand and he threw it at the fireball and both the ice ball and the fireball exploded into their respective elements, cancelling each other out.

"So that's how you kill people with your touch, Nazar." the man in the dojo said, "You used to be an Enlightened as well. You must have given up your Enlightenment to use your power to murder."

"Actually," Nazar said, "I became Enlightened in the first place knowing that I would gain extraordinary powers that I could use to continue my fun with killing."

"Your fun is over." Hideaki's friend said.

The man inside the dojo then put his arms up in the air, diagonal both ways from his body.

"Phoenix Renewal!" the man shouted as the rest of his dojo went up in flames and a gargantuan explosion arose from his body – forming a phoenix creature made of flames.

Everything in the area was burning; the city, his dojo, the surrounding cliffs and every bit of plant life in the area. Smoke covered the skies and the sun or clouds could not be seen.

"Fighting isn't fun." Nazar said, "Only killing…"

"Then I'll kill you!" said the man of the dojo, "Phoenix, attack!"

"Icy Grave!" Nazar shouted.

Water rose from the ground and surrounded Nazar; it then froze around him, creating an almost impenetrable looking shield.

Blizzard and firestorms were shooting through the air around them; it was almost as if the storms themselves were fighting one another alongside Nazar and the man of the dojo.

"Phoenix, attack!" he shouted and the phoenix shot five missiles of fire at the ice shield of Nazar.

Each ball melted a small piece of the ice, but just as the ice melted it simply froze again. The man attempted many more times to break through Nazar's shield, but he could not.

"Universal Chaos!" Hideaki screamed as a powerful and sharp winded tornado came from him.

The tornado slashed and slashed at the shield but it could only make small cuts with were simply revived just as they were made.

"Hideaki," the man said, "we can combine our powers!"

"Universal!" Hideaki screamed.

"Phoenix!" the man at the dojo screamed.

The sharp winds of Hideaki and the power of the man's phoenix combined and a pillar of fire formed as high as the sky.

Blizzards that may have been left in the area were defeated by the all-consuming fires of this powerful combination of cosmic energy.

"Pillar of fire," the man called out, "kill Nazar!"

The Pillar of Fire went forth and engulfed the shield of Nazar; the shield melted as if it were nothing.

"Why?" Nazar whispered to himself as he was enveloped in the flames.

"We've won!" Hideaki shouted.

"Not... yet." Nazar said, still somehow surviving in the flames.

"Frozen Death..." he said, and a ball of ice shot at the man of the dojo and froze him in a spiked ice block.

Nazar was then turned to ash by the Pillar of Fire and his ashes disappeared into the Pillar of Fire.

"Yoichi!" Hideaki screamed, "No, you can't die!"

Hideaki ran to his frozen friend, Yoichi.

"Universal Chaos!" he screamed and a tornado came forth, shaving the ice down to bits; however, Yoichi was still frozen within.

"There's nothing I can do." Hideaki said, falling to his knees crying over his frozen friend.

"I can help him..." said Skye with her tattoo glowing, "Love's Warmth!"

The words of Skye caused a heat wave to spiral around Yoichi and melt the ice encasing him. Her tattoo halted its glowing as she seemed to be coming out of a trance, probably induced by the tattoo.

"Thank you, girl." Yoichi said, "Fortunately, I'm immortal so I won't die from this. It is painful, though!"

"What?!" Hideaki said, "How could you still be immortal? You've chosen our side! Choosing sides takes your immortality from you…"

"No," Yoichi said, "Enlightenment is a contract and there are loopholes. I found one."

"What sort of loophole?" Hideaki asked.

"I didn't choose a side, Hideaki. I simply was having fun fighting Nazar, another immortal."

"How could that disgusting man still be Enlightened?!" Skye asked.

"He found the same loophole." Yoichi said, "If we decide to fight other immortals, knowing we cannot kill them, then it is just a harmless game not choosing a side. However, I'm not sure of what the loophole he found was."

"Maybe his powers over ice were not the powers of ice at all." Hideaki theorized, "Maybe it's the power to control time. He could have frozen his immortality into himself."

"Of course!" Yoichi said, "And the Pillar of Fire made his time flow again!"

"Okay..." Volf said, "Cosmic powers are weird."

"Idiot..." Skye said.

"My friend," Hideaki said, "We've come to gather the pieces of the Orb of Night. Leyb is too powerful for us to defeat."

"Are you sure?" Yoichi asked, "I think if we used the Pillar of Fire against Leyb that we could win..."

"Yoichi," Hideaki said, "You found these secret loopholes around the Cosmic Powers of the Old Ones, but you don't know the basic rules?"

"What do you mean?"

"Two Enlightened can only combine their powers once."

"Ah..." Yoichi said, "Maybe we can find a loophole..."

"I don't think so..." Hideaki said.

"Nonsense! Loopholes are everywhere!"

"Okay, enough about the loopholes, Yoichi! We know we can defeat Leyb with the Orb of Night, so we might as well gather the pieces! Where's yours?"

"I know, Hideaki!" Yoichi said with a smile, "I was just joking. Mine is right here on my necklace."

"You were joking while we're trapped in the middle of a city that's burning down in Cosmic Energy?!"

"Well, get used to it..." he said, "The only way to get four of the other pieces is to go into my dojo and find a key in the caverns below..."

"This time I hope you are joking..." Hideaki said.

"Uh... No." Yoichi said with a fake grin, "There are four keys scattered around the Eastern region that need to be found in order to open a secret vault on Middle Island."

"A secret vault?" Skye asked, "Is that where the rest of the pieces are?"

"No, only four of them are there." Yoichi said, "You'll have to find the others on your own."

"What do these keys look like, Yoichi?" Hideaki asked.

"They are spheres of four different Cosmic Souls."

"Cosmic Souls?" Volf asked.

"They are the souls of the Enlightened who have willingly given up their physical bodies in order to protect the pieces of the Orb of Night from being taken."

"Uh... What does that mean, exactly?" Volf asked.

"Idiot..." Skye said.

"Basically, the door to these four pieces is invincible to any attack until the four keys are brought to it. This makes it the safest vault for anything in the universe."

"After the key inside of your dojo, where are the other three?" Hideaki asked.

"They are living keys, Hideaki." Yoichi said, "If you need them then they will come to you."

"So... basically you don't know where they are?" Skye asked.

"Yes..." Yoichi said with his head looking down in shame.

"It's fine." Hideaki said, "He is right. The keys are living souls of the Enlightened, so they will come to us."

"Hurry, Hideaki!" Yoichi yelled, "Go into my dojo and find that key! I can feel a powerful evil Cosmic Energy approaching us... it's a general of Leyb."

"I see that I've lost my power to sense Cosmic Energy alongside my immortality..." Hideaki said.

"Yes, you've lost a lot of stuff. Now hurry and go inside!"

"What about you?" Volf asked.

"I'm immortal. I will have some fun with holding off this Evil Unenlightened."

"Unenlightened?" Hideaki asked.

"You don't know about them?" Yoichi asked, "They are the opposite of Enlightened.

They follow exactly the opposite of what the Old Ones tell us to do and they gain immortality... as vampires. This vampire is probably here for souls from the mass graves of bodies below."

"Ah, yes." Hideaki said, "I've heard of them. But not since I was a child... I saw a vampire named Obayifo..."

"Obayifo..." Yoichi repeated, "If you ever see Obayifo again, run..."

"Why?" Hideaki asked.

"He will someday be the one we Enlightened fight. He will someday be the one everyone fights for their existence; even the dead will fight him for their existence."

"Yoichi... You're an Old One, aren't you?" Hideaki asked.

Yoichi simply smiled and handed Hideaki his necklace with his piece of the Orb of Night attached. He turned and walked toward the graves at the edge of the town.

"Is he really an Old One, Hideaki?" Skye asked.

"I don't know, Skye..."

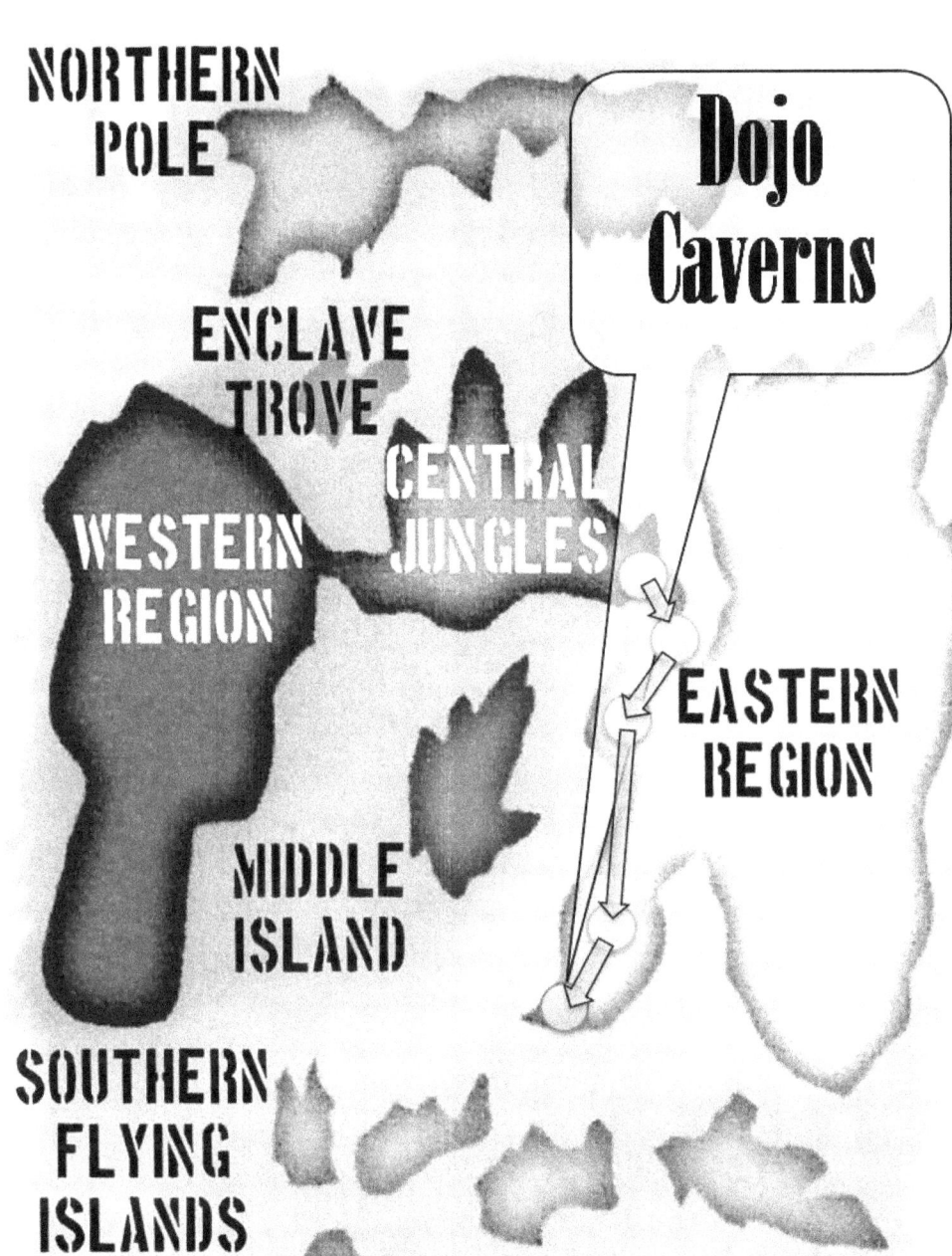

NORTHERN POLE

ENCLAVE TROVE

Dojo Caverns

CENTRAL JUNGLES

WESTERN REGION

EASTERN REGION

MIDDLE ISLAND

SOUTHERN FLYING ISLANDS

Sphere Zero

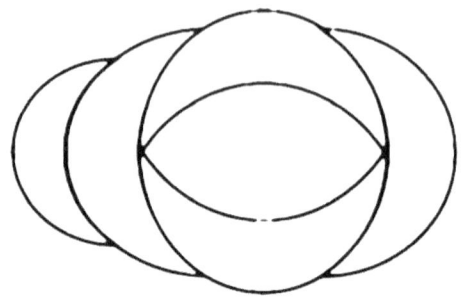

Chapter V: Yoko's Infernal Soul

Let's go into the dojo; we have to hurry, the entire dojo is going to collapse soon and we'll not be able to get in if we don't hurry."

"Doesn't that mean we'll be trapped in the caverns?!" Volf asked.

"Idiot!" Skye yelled, "Geez... Duh it means we'll be trapped! How stupid can you be?!"

"Skye!" Hideaki yelled.

"I know it means we'll be trapped," Volf said, "I was just making sure you guys knew... sorry."

"Sorry Volf... The heat is getting to me. We have to get inside... I'm not mad..."

The three of them then walked into the burning dojo – unknowing of where to look for the stairs down to the caverns.

Getting hotter every second, the group became increasingly agitated with one another. The dojo itself was feeling the heat and was about to collapse.

"We need to find the stairs!" Hideaki yelled to overpower the sound of the collapsing building.

"I can't see anything!" Volf said, "The heat is burning my eyes and it's hard to breathe in the smoke!"

"Yeah, I can't stand it, Hideaki!" Skye said with tears, covered in ash running down her face.

"Oh, dear…" Hideaki said, seeing Volf and Skye, "I shouldn't have dragged you two into this building. We should leave and find another way inside!"

"No!" Volf said, "We can't give up. We need that key!"

Hideaki looked down and sighed.

"Of course." Hideaki said, "Our health isn't as important as saving the entire region. But how can we find the stairs before we die?"

"I know where the stairs are." Skye said with her tattoo glowing, "My tattoo is talking to the key…"

"Oh, yeah!" Volf said, "The key's alive!"

"Of course!" Hideaki said, "Where are the stairs, Skye?!"

"This way!" she said as she led them to some stairs that led to the upper level.

"Skye!" Hideaki said, "I think the heat has gotten to you! These stairs go up, not down!"

"Now who's an idiot?" Volf said.

"You." Skye said, "Upstairs is another set of steps that leads into the caverns."

"Oh," Volf said, "right. I knew that..."

"Idiot..."

"Let's go, you two!" Hideaki yelled.

They all ran up the steps and saw an area that looked completely different than the wood in the surrounding area; a set of stone steps leading downward into a dungeon like area.

"Hurry!" Skye yelled.

Rushing down into the dungeons, they heard the sound of the dojo finally collapsing and debris began to fall down the steps alongside them.

"This isn't good." Hideaki said, "It looks like the fires will spread to these dungeons, too..."

"Don't worry." Skye said with a still-glowing tattoo, "I know we'll make it."

"Very well, Skye..." Hideaki said cautiously.

"So, where are we going, Skye?"

"Just keep following me..." she said, "I'm not sure where the key is, but I know I'm going the right way..."

"Creepy..." Volf said.

"Idiot..." Skye said with a dull voice and eyes staring straight ahead of her.

Walking down the hallway, they could hear the sounds of the ceiling cracking slowly; they didn't worry about it at first, because they couldn't see the cracks, but it became worse and worse.

"Hideaki," Volf said, "Should we be hurrying it up, more?"

"Like I said before, the fires could spread to these dungeons... Cosmic energy into fire isn't a very good thing... it could burn for thousands of years before it burns out."

"Wow..." Volf said.

"Yes." Skye said lifelessly, "Wow."

"Hm..." Hideaki muttered.

Just then, the ceiling began to show signs of wear and huge cracks began to appear; red light could be seen shining through the holes and crack all over the place.

"We need to hurry, Skye!" Volf said.

"Skye," Hideaki said, "Can you go any faster, please?!"

"No." Skye responded, "I need to go slowly so I can talk to the key... It's hard to get directions from it, but I can still get them... if we relax and go at a modest pace..."

"Modest pace?!" Hideaki shouted, "We're about to die! We need to go faster!"

"Yes." Skye said, "Faster... Faster!"

Skye's tattoo finally stopped glowing and she took a deep breath of relief.

"Finally, I can control myself again!"

"You weren't controlling yourself?" Volf asked.

"Oh my Old Ones!" she shouted, "You! Are! An! Idiot!"

"That's why I thought you were controlling yourself..." he said, "You still called me an idiot when you were acting kind of weird..."

"Okay..." she said, "I admit I could control myself a little bit, but the tattoo—"

"Skye," Hideaki interrupted, "I think your tattoo may be evil..."

"It's not evil!" she shouted, "It was just trying to help... it didn't take full control of me. It could easily take me over if it wanted... It never controls my beliefs, only my body!"

"So that's why you still called me an idiot..."

"Yeah..." she said, "Anyway, I know where to go now, so let's run before this entire place collapses!"

They began running for their lives as the ceiling was falling down upon them; the ceiling was only about half a meter from their heads, so they needed to be very careful about falling pieces.

"How is it that you know exactly where the key is now, Skye?" Volf asked.

"What do you mean?"

"Before when the tattoo was controlling you..." Volf continued, "you said that you had to relax and go at a modest pace, and that you didn't know where the key was. Now you can run and you do know where the key is?"

"The tattoo was having trouble using my body to talk to the key, so it taught me how to and let me control myself again."

"Ah!" Hideaki said, "That seems like a very wise decision."

"So," Skye shouted trying to overpower the sound of the crumbling dungeon, "do you still think it's evil?!

"No," Hideaki said, "I think I just misunderstood its intentions. I believe that tattoo may be a part of something far greater... and it may be more powerful than the Orb of Night."

"It is." Skye said.

"How do you know that, Skye?" Hideaki asked.

"I can't tell you..." she said, "I made a Cosmic promise to the tattoo..."

"You made a Cosmic promise?!" he asked, "Those are dangerous, Skye! If you fail to uphold the bargain, the Ruler of Death will come for you and use the Universal Complete Annihilation power on you…"

"I know…" she said.

"How much do you know about Cosmic energy?!" Hideaki asked.

"More than you…" she responded.

Hideaki stayed in silence at that moment, contemplating the possibility that this young girl could know more than him about Cosmic energy.

Flames were beginning to shoot down from the cracking; the group began to run faster and faster to escape the fires.

Leading the other two, Skye knew about an alternate route from her current one; this alternate route would take them safely downward from the current level where they could avoid the inferno.

Skye stayed silent about the fact that she was taking an alternate route, because she knew they would be all-for going lower into the ground at this point.

Downstairs they traveled through a large hall of sorts; there were thousands of pillars seen in every direction – each one-hundred times the size of Yoichi's dojo-mansion.

Looking up they could see a ceiling that was around two kilometers high. They had walked down a long staircase for hours upon hours, yet the fires could still be seen from this subterranean palace of sorts.

Every direction they looked seemed to go for kilometers; this palace might very well stretch throughout the entire Eastern region.

"Where are we?" Hideaki asked."

"I'm not sure." Skye said, "I just know that this is the way to the key."

"So not even the key knows where we are?" Volf asked.

"Nope." Skye said, "It doesn't matter where we are, anyway. We just need to make sure that we go on the right path to get the key."

"Yeah…"

"Of course…"

"What was that, guys?" she asked.

"Nothing, Skye." Hideaki said.

"Oh, okay." She said.

"What an idiot!" Volf whispered to Hideaki, "She didn't hear us."

"I heard that, idiot!"

"Heard… what?" Volf said in a guilty voice.

"Idiot…" she said.

Hideaki snickered at the two of them in their immaturity.

"You realize I could lead you to the wrong place, right Hideaki!"

"Umh... I wasn't laughing at you two..."

"Really?" she asked sarcastically.

"Fine... I'll shut up."

"Good." She said.

"These kids really need to learn to respect their elders and they..." he continued to mutter incomprehensibly.

The three of them continued through the wondrous palace; they finally came to a door with a strange statue next to it.

"Statue," Skye said, "give us your test so we can go inside."

"What are you talking about, Skye?" Volf asked.

"You'll see... idiot."

"Can you please stop calling me that?"

"Yes."

"Thanks, Skye."

"Idiot."

"Hey!"

"You asked if I 'can' stop."

"Will you please stop?"

"Stop what?"

"Oh my... Never mind, Skye..."

"Statue!"

"I heard you the first time, girl." It said, "I waited for your amusing conversation to end."

"Okay..." she said, "So what's the test?"

"The test is a question." The statue said.

"So what is the question?"

"Which of you five is the most powerful?"

"Five?" Volf asked.

"Yes." The statue said.

"But there are only three of us." Volf responded.

"Then I guess you will fail this test." the statue teased.

"Okay..." Volf said, "Hideaki, you must be the most powerful!"

"No." Hideaki said, "Skye's tattoo is the most powerful. It is alive like Skye, you and I."

"Oh!" Volf said, "That makes sense!"

"Statue," Skye said, "my tattoo is the most powerful of us."

"That is correct." the statue said as the door opened, "You may enter the door, now."

"Wait... Skye, you, the tattoo and I... That's four of us. Then who's the fifth person?"

"Idiot..." Skye said, "The Orb of Night is."

"Oh..."

Inside they went; here they saw the first of the four keys. It was red like the fire of Yoichi.

"I wonder who this Enlightened was…" Skye said.

"It was most likely Yoichi's sister," Hideaki said, "Yoko."

"Can't you ask the thing's name?" Volf asked.

"No," Skye said, "The soul doesn't remember anything from its physical body's life."

"Ah," Hideaki said, "Of course. They must give up their physical bodies and even their entire physical lives to become this way. The only thing left of them is this shell for their Soul energy."
"Okay…" Volf said, "First there's Cosmic energy… now Soul energy?"

"Yes, Volf." Hideaki said, "Cosmic power comes from the world around us – Soul power comes from within. The more we follow the ways of the Old Ones the more powerful our Soul power is, but the same now seems to be true if you do the exact opposite of the Old Ones…"

"Yeah," Skye said, "Vampires, like what Yoichi told us about. But, vampires are the exact opposite; they have given up their souls to have an immortal and undying body."

"That makes sense, Skye." Hideaki said, "Did the tattoo tell you this?"

"Yeah…" she said, "I know a lot more about energy, too… There are more kinds of energy in the universe. Death energy, for instance. Aether energy…"

"You know about Aether energy?"

"Yeah." She said, "It could be the most powerful of them all."

"Don't tell anyone about this, Skye!" Hideaki said.

"I won't." she responded.

"Wait." Volf said, "What's going on?"

"Idiot." Skye said.

"I'm not an idiot!"

"Right." Skye said, "Just like you know what we were talking about."

"Whatever," Volf said, "You just think you're smart because you know about energy and stuff… You wouldn't even know it if it wasn't for that tattoo giving you all the answers."

"Yeah, I'm sorry Volf…" she said, "I'm just kind of hostile to you all the time… My competitiveness is just because everyone has always been against me because of my tattoo… No one has ever been nice to me like you. Sorry if I call you names, but I really do appreciate your kindness… and your intelligence."

"You think I'm smart?"

"No." she said, "But I do appreciate the intelligence you do have… What I mean is that you know how to be nice, but I don't. You're intelligent in that way…"

"Oh…" Volf said, "Thank you, I guess…"

"Enough chatting." Hideaki said, "Grab the Key and we'll leave, now."

"Okay." Skye said as she picked up the orb.

"There is a piece here…" she said.

"What?" Volf asked.

"A piece of the Orb of Night here…"

"Where?" Hideaki asked.

"Inside of the key…"

"Of course!" Hideaki said, "When Yoko gave up her physical body, her Soul energy and the Aether energy must have combined together…"

"So, " Volf said, "Aether energy is the energy of the Orb of Night?"

"Yes, "Hideaki said, "and of the Orb of Night exclusively. No other object on our planet has this strange energy."

"What should we do about the piece inside of Yoko's soul?" Skye asked.

"Once we gather the Keys and go to Middle Island to open the vault… Hopefully it'll separate from the Aether energy and allow us to take the piece out without destroying her soul." Hideaki said.

"Good plan!" Volf said, "Now, how do we get out of here?"

"I'll ask the Key." Skye said.

"You really need to teach us how to do that, Skye…" Hideaki said.

"It wouldn't be hard, actually." she said, "You only have to touch my forehead to learn how to speak to the Keys."

"Very well." Hideaki said, "Volf, you learn it first. Tap the tattoo."

"Okay…"

Volf touched her tattoo and it glowed briefly.

"It didn't do anything." He said.

"Seriously?" Skye asked.

"No, I'm just kidding. I can talk to the keys, now. How are ya' doin, Yoko?!"

"Idiot…" Yoko said.

"Hey…" Volf said, "Why does everyone think I'm an idiot?"

"What just happened?" Hideaki asked.

"Nothing!" Volf said, "Just touch the friggin' tattoo, already…"

"Very well…"

Hideaki put his palm against the tattoo and it glowed briefly once again.

"I understand, Yoko." he said, "Volf is kind of an idiot."

"Oh come on!" Volf said.

"We're just messing with you." Yoko said, "But seriously, the exits right over there in the back of the room. Just touch that statue outside the room's nose and it'll open the door."

"Okay." Volf said as he walked out of the room, "I'm touching the nose and I don't think it's doing anything..."

"I was just messing with you, Volf." Yoko said, "You actually have to pull its tail."

Volf took a deep breath in annoyance and pulled the tail – which also did nothing.

Yoko began to laugh at him.

"I was just messing with you again." Yoko said, "I can just open the door without you doing anything."

"Seriously?!" he asked.

"Yep." She responded as the door opened itself.

"Seriously..." Volf muttered as he marched out the door.

Skye and Yoko were snarling as they walked behind him.

"Immature children," Hideaki said, "all of you..."

"Yoko," Skye said, "How old are you?"

"How... old?" Yoko asked.

"Idiot!" Volf said, "You don't know what 'how old' means?"

"I don't understand..." Yoko responded...

After arguing back and forth about whom was smarter for hours, they finally reached the top of the steps.

Upstairs was another door which Yoko opened for them; outside were the mass graves, Yoichi and a vampire. They exited and the door closed behind them...

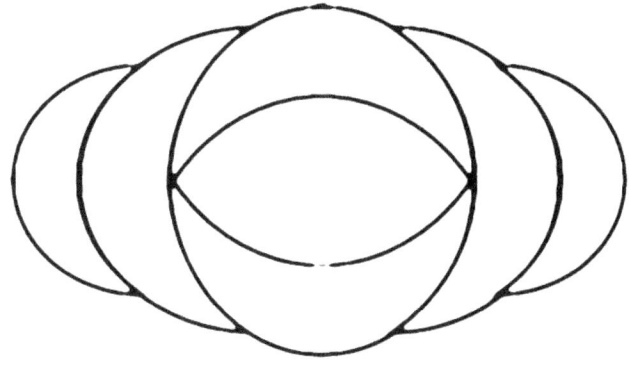

Chapter VI: Midnight Vampire

Yoichi shot fireball after fireball at the vampire; each one was successful in ripping it apart, but the vampire simply regenerated its body from each shot.

"It's too dark..." Hideaki said, "Yoko, can you tell who it is?"

Yoko stayed silent at his question.

"She's asleep." Skye said, "Her Soul energy was used up for now by opening those doors for us."

"I'm sure all of that arguing up the steps didn't help either..." Hideaki said.

"It's that idiot Volf's fault..." Skye said.

"Anyway..." Hideaki said, "Let's get a closer look at the vampire and see why Yoichi's powers aren't affecting it.

"They can't hurt it now," Skye said, "Vampires regenerate at nighttime."

"That's scary…" Volf said, "Should we run, then?"

"Maybe, Volf." She said, "It would probably be the smartest thing to do…"

Walking closer to the Vampire, Skye finally saw its face.

"Usha…" Skye said.

"What?" Hideaki asked.

"General Usha!" Skye said, "She was a vampire all along!"

"Of course!" Hideaki said, "She just didn't revive until it was nighttime after I thought I killed her."

"Okay…" Volf said, "Now I just want to leave. I already had nightmares about her before I knew she was a vampire."

"Well," Skye said, "she did torture you and almost kill you. Anyone would have nightmares of that…"

"Skye, Volf," Hideaki said, "we really should leave…"

"What about Yoichi?" Volf asked.

"He is powerful." Hideaki assumed, "He should be able to handle himself."

"I don't think so." Skye said, "Look…"

Skye pointed at Usha who was encroaching upon Yoichi; he could do nothing to stop her advance.

"Vampire!" he yelled as threw another fireball, "You have no right to live with your disgusting ways!"

"So," Usha said, "are you done attacking me, yet? Everything you're doing is pointless."

"No," Yoichi said, "I know how to kill a vampire. I'm just waiting until day I can melt you with the sun!"

"But that's so long from now." Usha said, "You can't last much longer."

"You're right." Yoichi said cunningly, "So I'll just make another sun!"

"Impossible!" Usha yelled.

"Foxfire!" he shouted as he threw a large ball of fire into the sky, "Plasma Rain!"

"No!" Usha screamed, "Please stop!"

"You asked too late." Yoichi said.

Balls of plasma as hot as the sun itself began to rain upon the land; in every direction the terrain turned to magma.

Corpses in the mass graves began to melt under the heat of this terrible attack. Light from the plasma smothered the darkness of the night.

"Please!" Usha begged, "Obayifo!"

"Obayifo?!" Yoichi said, "Don't call for that monster, Usha! I'll spare you if you leave him out of this!"

"You asked too late!" Usha said, "Black Hole Portal!"

When Usha yelled a black hole appeared in the sky; this dark tear in the sky ripped the artificial Foxfire sun apart and cooled the land.

Darkness reigned once again, unfortunately this time it was even darker than before. The portal stole the light of the moon and the stars.

"Obayifo," Usha said, "Help me Dark Saint!"

Lightning shot from Usha's arms as she raised them into the air. Spreading across the sky like a terrible storm, the portal took every bit of her lightning and lit itself up.

"Usha…" said a voice from the portal, "I can't help you yet. You need more Soul energy."

"But I have the bodies of thousands, here!" Usha said.

"No," Yoichi said, "look again, Usha. My foxfire melted those bodies and their Soul energy was sent off to the Ruler of Death."

"Fine." Usha said, "But from the looks of it, your control over the Cosmic energy is running out."

"Only a little." Yoichi said, "I'm still more powerful than you will ever be. And we're both immortal; what could we do to harm one another? Unless I used my Foxfire again; I think I have just enough energy to do so…"

"No you can't!" Usha said, "You can't use your power with my portal opened!"

"That's true." Yoichi said, "But the portal won't last forever. Your concentration of Cosmic energy is running out and your Soul energy seems to be almost nil. You should go now, before I change my mind."

"Go!" Obayifo said from the portal, "The fool gives you a chance to live. He has to honor his promise like any other thoughtless Enlightened."

"Okay," Usha said, "but before I go... Universal Complete Annihilation!"

Darkness shot from Usha's fingertip and struck Yoichi; his immortality protected him from immediate death, but smoke encased his body and only strange lights could be seen coming from within.

"Yoichi!" Hideaki shouted and ran toward him.

"Those three..." Usha said while backing away, "I'll take my leave."

Usha turned and ran to the nearby forest, leaving Yoichi encased in the ultimate power of Death.

"What happened?" Hideaki asked.

"He is being tested." Skye said, "Enlightened can't be killed by that power, so they're tested to make sure that they're really Enlightened..."

"But, I truly thought that Yoichi was an Old One..." Hideaki said, "Not just an Enlightened."

"Old Ones are the same as us." Skye said, "They have to be an Enlightened or a Vampire to be immortal…"

"Well then," Hideaki said, "what kind of test is Yoichi going through?"

"I don't know." Skye said, "The tattoo is sleeping just like Yoko."

"Do all magical things sleep right now?" Hideaki asked rudely.

"Yes." Skye said, "This would be the time most things sleep… it's midnight."

"Right…" Hideaki said, "Sorry, Skye. I'm not thinking at all right now."

"It's fine, Hideaki."

"Can we help him at all?" Volf asked.

"No." Skye said, "If you touch that cluster of smoke, you'll die instead."

"So," Volf said, "Technically we could help him…"

"If you want to die!" she said, "Idiot."

"Still… You said we couldn't help him!"

"Oh we can help him!" she said sarcastically, "Just like we can decide to never eat or drink water. Idiot!"

"Please," Hideaki said, "be quiet. I am very restless in this situation."

"He'll probably be out soon." Skye said, "I know he'll make it. If he is an Old One, he definitely knows how to be Enlightened."

"Of course…" Hideaki said.

Hours rolled by after their conversation and the sun came out; Volf had fallen asleep, but Hideaki and Skye stayed awake during the whole ordeal.

"Phoenix Renewal!" Yoichi shouted from within the smoke.

Yoichi's phoenix of flames them consumed the smoke and nothing was left of it. Yoichi walked out unharmed and untouched.

"Yoichi!" Hideaki said.

"Hideaki! You waited for me here this whole time?"

"Both of us did," Skye said, "but that idiot Volf fell asleep..."

"No," Yoichi said, "he's the only smart one. He didn't get himself all worried about something he couldn't help with. Now, he'll be the only one of us that is well rested!"

"But... He just acted like he didn't care!" Skye said.

"Nonsense!" Yoichi said, "He just knew that he couldn't help, but he knew what he could do – sleep!"

"Nevertheless," Hideaki said, "what sort of horrible tests did it put you through!?"

"Well... After sitting there in that cloud of black smoke for hours, I realized that the test was just to escape without being killed – which only an immortal could do!"

"So, it was painless?" Skye asked.

"Yep!"

"And you could have done that last night?" Hideaki asked.

"Yeah!"

"That means I didn't have to sit here worrying all night?!" Hideaki asked.

"Well..." Yoichi said, "You could have just been like Volf over there and slept..."

"Whatever..." Hideaki said.

"Now you're just acting like a child, Hideaki!"

"I suppose I am. I'm sorry, but I am old and tired. I have lost my immortality and youth in this war..."

"Don't worry, Hideaki." Yoichi said, "Someday you won't have to worry about age ever again."

"Yes, I know... I'm going to die."

"That's not what I meant, Hideaki. Someday, if everything works out then everyone will be immortal. There will be no more death or suffering."

"How?" he asked.

"Don't worry." Yoichi said as he turned and walked toward the south, "I am going to the Southern Flying Islands. Someday, you should come and visit me. You will know when the time is right for the visit."

"How will I know?" Hideaki asked.

"Well..." Yoichi said, "Seeing as how the only way to get on top of the magical flying islands is with either Energy powers of some kind or powerful technology... I'd say you'll know when you have the ability to get there!"

"Right..." Hideaki said, "But how do you get–"

"Phoenix Renewal!" Yoichi shouted and his phoenix sprouted out from beneath him. It carried him away into the southern skies and to the Flying Islands.

"Now what?" Skye asked.

"First of all," Volf said from behind, "I just found another piece of the Orb of Night!"

"Where?!" Skye asked.

"It was on Usha's ear... that she left on the ground."

"Ew!" she shouted, "She used it as an earring?!"

"That's not good!" Hideaki said.

"I know!" Skye said, "That would look terrible on her!"

"Not that, Skye!" he said, "If she had one of them as an earring, than she was probably wearing another as an earring on her other ear."

"So now we have to find her?"

"Yes," Hideaki said, "we need to go East. That is the way that she fled."

"Should I take her ear?" Volf asked.

"Ew!" Skye shouted, "Why would we do that, idiot?!"

"Because," Volf said, "we could trade it for the other earring!"

"She's not that stupid!" Skye said.

"Maybe she is!" Hideaki said, "She may not know that the earrings have powerful energies within them."

"Good point." Skye said.

"We're done talking." Hideaki said, "Let's go east."

Setting out they knew they would be heading straight through the path of two of his generals: Kione and Ayé – a couple of married crooks – they had a tough fight ahead.

NORTHERN POLE

Corrupt City

ENCLAVE TROVE

CENTRAL JUNGLES

WESTERN REGION

EASTERN REGION

MIDDLE ISLAND

SOUTHERN FLYING ISLANDS

Sphere Zero

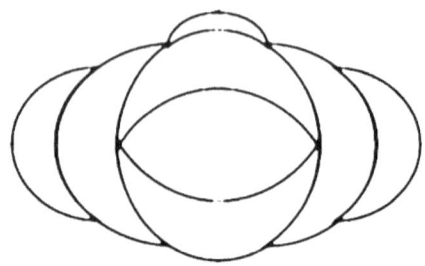

Chapter VII: Partners in Crime

Reaching a large city to the Northeast of Yoichi's dojo, the group decided to rest after almost a week of traveling after facing Usha. It looked to be a still a peaceful town, unfound by Leyb's armies as of yet.

Streets were bustling with noise and lights even during the night; the group found an inn where they decided to stay.

"I don't have any money." Skye said.

"I do!" Volf said.

"You don't need to pay." Hideaki said, "Another of my Enlightened friends owns this inn."

"Cool!" Skye said.

"Who is it?" Volf asked.

"You'll see when we get inside."

Walking inside they noticed that the inn was empty; things inside the inn had been ripped apart and things were missing all throughout the store.

"What happened?" Hideaki asked himself, "This town was taken over by Leyb!"

"What?!" Skye said.

"The town must be under his control." He said.

"Why do you say that?" Volf asked.

"There is a note on the counter, there." Hideaki said.

"*Dear visitor*," it read, "*this inn has been temporarily shut down by the wills of our new king and queen: Kione and Ayé. It will be back in business when we've found a more suitable inn keeper.*"

"Who are Kione and Ayé?" Volf asked.

"Two of Leyb's generals." Hideaki said, "They're married."

"Two of Leyb's generals are married?" Skye asked, "I just thought they were all heartless monsters, but they're actually in love with each other?"

"I don't think it is love." Hideaki said, "I think it is a marriage between two very disturbed people who found each other to be... very similar."

"Disturbed..." Volf said, "Sounds like all of Leyb's generals."

"It does." Hideaki said, "Now we need to find my Enlightened friend."

"Do you think he's still alive?" Volf asked, "Nazar couldn't even get into Yoichi's house because he was Enlightened, why could they get in here?"

"Because it's an inn." Skye said.

"Oh, right..." Volf said, "I know, I'm an idiot."

"I wasn't going to say that." Skye said, "But it's still true."

"Whatever..."

"That's where he is!" Hideaki shouted, "The capital building in the center of town has a jail."

"How do you know that?" Skye asked.

"I see a note here left by my friend."

"*Hideaki,*" it read, "*I know you're coming here. I lost my immortality. I know it sounds bad, but I did it for a good reason. The guards were about to kill a young child, but I couldn't allow it. I had to step in and save her. I beat the guards that were around her and came into here; I hid this note under the counter like I had said I would do if I was ever in danger. I knew you'd find the note. The guards will be coming for me. Everyone in town knows what I've done and they don't want to report me, but they have no choice. I'm going to be waiting for you in the prison, Hideaki.*"

"My friend is waiting for us." Hideaki said, "Let's go get her out of there."

"Hideaki," Skye said, "with all due respect we just can't go tonight. We need to rest up and then go tomorrow night."

"Yes," Hideaki said, "I suppose you're right. I let my friendship with her cloud my judgment..."

"Her?" Volf asked.

"Yes," Hideaki said, "it is a female. Is there something you have against that?"

"I think he's asking if you might think of her as more than a friend..." Skye said.

"What?" Hideaki asked, "No! Of course not."

"Idiot." Skye said, "You upset Hideaki!"

"Sorry," Volf said, "but I still think you like her more than you're saying."

"Impossible!" Hideaki said, "Enlightened are not allowed to be romantically involved with one another..."

"Well," Skye said, "you're not immortal anymore, so it wouldn't hurt."

"You two don't understand." Hideaki said.

"I think we do." Volf said.

"Yeah," Skye said, "I think we understand that you're trying to hide your feelings for her!"

"You imbeciles!" Hideaki said, "She's my mother!"

"You get romantic with your mom?!" Volf asked.

"Idiot!" Skye said, "Just shut up..."

"You thought it, too..."

"Not with his mom!"

"Enough!" Hideaki said, "We'll rescue my mother tomorrow. For now, we'll stay here in my family's inn."

"Your family's inn?" Volf asked.

"Yes." Hideaki said, "My family has owned this inn for thousands of years. My mother and I are the only ones who have run the inn for the past fifty-thousand years."

"Wait..." Skye said, "Are you saying that you're fifty-thousand years old?"

"No." Hideaki responded.

"Oh, okay." Volf said, "That sounded a bit too old..."

"Idiot!" Skye said, "Just shut up, Volf!"

"Okay..."

"Actually," Hideaki said, "I'm sixty-two-thousand three-hundred and eight years old, Volf."

"Wow!" Skye said, "You've been alive for a long time, Hideaki. What's it like living for so long?"

"Boring!" he said, "I've done everything a million times!"

"Well," Volf said, "I'm going to bed, now."

"What?!" Skye said, "Don't you want to know more about Hideaki's really huge lifetime?!"

"Nah." Volf said, "I'm tired."

"I think I'll be going to bed now, too." Hideaki said.

"Seriously?" Skye said, "Guys are so simple..."

Sleeping well, they felt great about the rescue for the next night. Wasting time until night though was the hard part.

Hideaki decided that it was best for them to stay inside for the remainder of the time between waking up and the rescue.

Countless hours went by and the sun finally set. After gathering supplies, Hideaki remembered something.

"Skye! Volf!" he said, "I remember a secret entrance into the jail that my mother told me about!"

"Where is it?" Skye asked.

"Downstairs!"

"Seriously?" Skye asked, "You mean we could have been breaking into the jail this entire day and still been secretive?!"

"Maybe..." Hideaki said.

"Whatever." Skye said angrily, "Let's just go before I kill you both out of boredom..."

Descending into the basement they ran into cobwebs and large spiders as tall as half their bodies; these creatures were afraid of light so they ran when the upstairs door was open.

Unfortunately, the spiders were not afraid of humans. Stalking the group, they waited for an opportune time to attack their prey.

"These things are scary…" Skye said.

"I agree…" Hideaki said, "Planet Crumbler!"

At the words of Hideaki, a small orb appeared at the end of Hideaki's beard, which was suspended in front of him. It created light for them.

"What was that Cosmic power?" Skye asked.

"Planet Crumbler is a power that could be concentrated enough to create a blast strong enough to enter into a planet's core and destabilize it." Hideaki responded.

"Can you teach me that?" Volf asked.

"If we ever find another peaceful day in our lives I will." Hideaki said.

Continuing through the basement they found a single torch, which the spiders avoided like the plague; they had even covered the area in webs to hide the light.

"Now," Hideaki said, "I'll just turn this torch down and the secret door will open."

Turning the torch counter-clockwise he turned the torch upside down and the oil began to pour onto the floor.

Just as it hit the floor, the walls all lit up in the basement and the spiders began to run in about in panic of the omniscient light.

Opening aside the torch was a small door, only big enough to fit one person in at a time. The hallway inside seemed to stretch forever.

"This will take us to the jail and into one of the cells." Hideaki said.

Walking for three hours in this undersized passage they made it to the entrance door for the jail; Hideaki pushed it forward and it fell to the ground and shattered.

"Oops!" he said.

"Who cares!" Skye shouted, "I just want out of this chamber! I hate small places like this!"

"It's not that bad." Volf said, "At least no one can attack you with you in the middle of us."

"Shut up, idiot!"

Getting out of the cramped chamber was a relief to all of them, but for Skye the most. Looking around they saw that they were in an abandoned area of the jail.

"Come on." Hideaki said, "I think this cell is unlocked."

Hideaki led them to the cell door and they exited into the corridors. From here, he led them to the left and through many corridors until they finally found the area where they held new inmates.

"There she is!" Hideaki said.

"That young woman?" Skye asked, "I thought she would look older…"

"She became immortal at a very young age." Hideaki said.

"So you look young forever if you become immortal when you're young?"

"Yes." Hideaki said.

"I guess you didn't get immortal so young then, Hideaki." Volf said.

Hideaki rolled his eyes at Volf and Skye looked at with confused eyes.

"Why do you always say stupid things, Volf?" she asked.

"Sorry…"

"It's fine." Skye said, "Let's just rescue his mom."

"Yeah." Volf said, "What's her name, anyway?"

"Amaya." Hideaki said.

"That's a beautiful name!" Skye said.

"There's no time for this now." Hideaki said, "We need to rescue her now. I heard the guards saying they're going to kill her!"

Hideaki jumped from around the corner from which they were looking and blasted them away.

"Universal Chaos!" he shouted.

Sharp winds chopped the soldiers to pieces and Hideaki looked at his mother behind bars nearby.

"Hideaki!" Amaya said, "I knew you'd come."

"Mother," he said, "can you get yourself out of there?"

"Yes, dear." She said, "Moon's Gravity!"

Cosmic energies became very concentrated around her and the gravity of the moon itself bent the bars of her cell.

"Why didn't you just escape by yourself?" Skye asked, "In fact, why did you let them capture you at all?"

"Well, dear." Amaya said, "Kione's wife, Ayé has a strange staff with an orb on the end. It's invincible…"

"Of course!" Hideaki said, "It's another Key, Skye!"

"So now we have to fight these two generals?" Skye asked.

"Yes," Hideaki said, "I suppose so."

"I'll help you out, Hideaki." Amaya said, "But I'll be staying in town one you leave."

"Very well, mother." Hideaki said, "I'd appreciate your help."

"My help?" Amaya asked, "I appreciate your help in rescuing me!"

"Enough pleasantries, mother." Hideaki said, "We need to find Kione and Ayé."

"That's easy." Amaya said, "They're so prideful that they always sit in the front entrance of Capital Hall. They think they're invincible with that magical orb. Or key or whatever it is."

"It's a soul of an Enlightened." Volf said, "There are four of them that gave up their bodies to become invincible guardians of a door to four of the pieces of the Orb of Night."

"Ah!" Amaya said, "So you're gathering the Orb of Night together. What could possibly drive you to do something that desperate?"

"Leyb's armies... They're too powerful."

"Are you sure there's no other option?" Amaya asked.

"We've already gathered some of the pieces and I've given up my immortality because of this..."

"You did what?!" she asked.

"We've gathered some of the–"

"That's not what I meant! You've lost your immortality, too?"

"Yes, mother." Hideaki said, "I gave it up to fight Leyb's armies."

"Then our old inn will finally be abandoned." She said, "We've both lost our immortality and our family will die out."

"Mother," Hideaki said, "your body is still young and you could still get married and have a large family with your time left."

"Right!" she said, "Too bad you waited so long to become Enlightened, Hideaki. I don't want to see you die before I do."

"We'll catch up later, mother." He said, "Let's go pay Kione and Ayé a visit. Will you show us the way?"

"Sure, Hideaki." She said.

Amaya led them through the jail and they fought many other small bands of guards along the way. At the end of the hallways was a spiral staircase leading upward.

"Upstairs is the room where Kione and Ayé stay." She said, "We'll have to fight them there."

Upstairs they went and just as they saw Kione and Ayé – Kione and Ayé saw them.

"Guards!" Ayé yelled, "Intruders from the jail staircase!"

The few guards in the area rushed at the group.

"Universal Chaos!" Hideaki screamed and his sharp winds chopped a few of them to shreds.

"Universal Chaos!" Volf yelled and his winds simply knocked down his targets.

"Thunderstorm Shock Therapy!" Amaya yelled and lightning shot from her fingertips, striking any remaining soldiers.

"Enlightened!" Kione yelled, "Let's run, Ayé!"

Kione and Ayé then made a run for it; they got out the front exit and the group followed them.

Running through the town the group did not come upon any resistance; instead, the crowds were cheering at the sight of Kione and Ayé fleeing from town.

Stopping at the outskirts of town, the group saw Kione and Ayé on a moving train that carried them off into the distance.

"No!" Hideaki said, "We can't lose that Key!"

"You won't." Amaya said, "Moon's Gravity!"

Her power began pulling at the staff and Key at its end; Ayé tried to hold on with it as best she could.

"Kione!" Ayé said, "They're using some weird powers to try and pull the staff from me!"

Kione grabbed hold of the staff with her and they were successful in keeping it; fortunately, the Key separated from the staff and flew far away and into Amaya's hand.

"That was amazing, Amaya!" Skye said.

"Thanks."

"Mother, I..."

"I know." She said, "I know you need to leave. Here's the key."

"No," Hideaki said, "that's not it... I haven't been kind to you during this visit and I'm sorry. I haven't told you this yet... I love you, mother."

"I love you too, Hideaki!"

Amaya put her arms around her son to give him a large hug; she hadn't given her son a hug in centuries.

"Hideaki," Amaya said with tears, "why haven't you visited for so long? It's been... almost a thousand years."

"I know, mother." He said, "I'm sorry. I'll come visit you again once this war is over. And I promise to give you a hug just like today."

"Good." Amaya said, "Now, I have a family to start."

"Actually," Skye said, "you don't lose your Enlightenment when you save a young child. That is why you think you lost your immortality, right?"

"Yes... Are you sure about that, though?" she asked.

"Skye is the most knowledgeable person on the Enlightened in the world." Hideaki said.

"Thanks, Hideaki."

"Are you Enlightened, Skye?" Amaya asked.

"No," she said, "I just... never mind."

"She has a magical tattoo on her forehead that taught her everything!" Volf blurted out.

"Idiot..." Skye said.

"Why does it matter, Skye?" she asked, "Do you feel like the tattoo makes you less of a person? It doesn't. I can tell that you are a wonderful person."

"Thank you, Amaya." Skye said, "That means more to me than anything my own mother ever said to me..."

"Then consider me your mother!"

"Uhm... I can't do that." Skye said, "You just look too young."

"Yeah," Amaya said, "I do look about as young as you do... Maybe younger."

"You don't look younger!" Skye shouted, "You're old!"

"Alright, alright." Amaya said, "I was just joking!"

"We need to go." Hideaki said, "We still need to find Usha and get her piece of the Orb of Night."

"Alright." Amaya said, "I love you Hideaki! It was nice to meet you, Skye! And whoever you are... Idiot, was it?"

"I'm not an idiot!" Volf said, "It's Volf..."

"Oh… Right. Volf! It was nice to meet you, too."

Amaya turned and walked back to town and the three heroes walked northeastwardly, looking for Usha and the married couple.

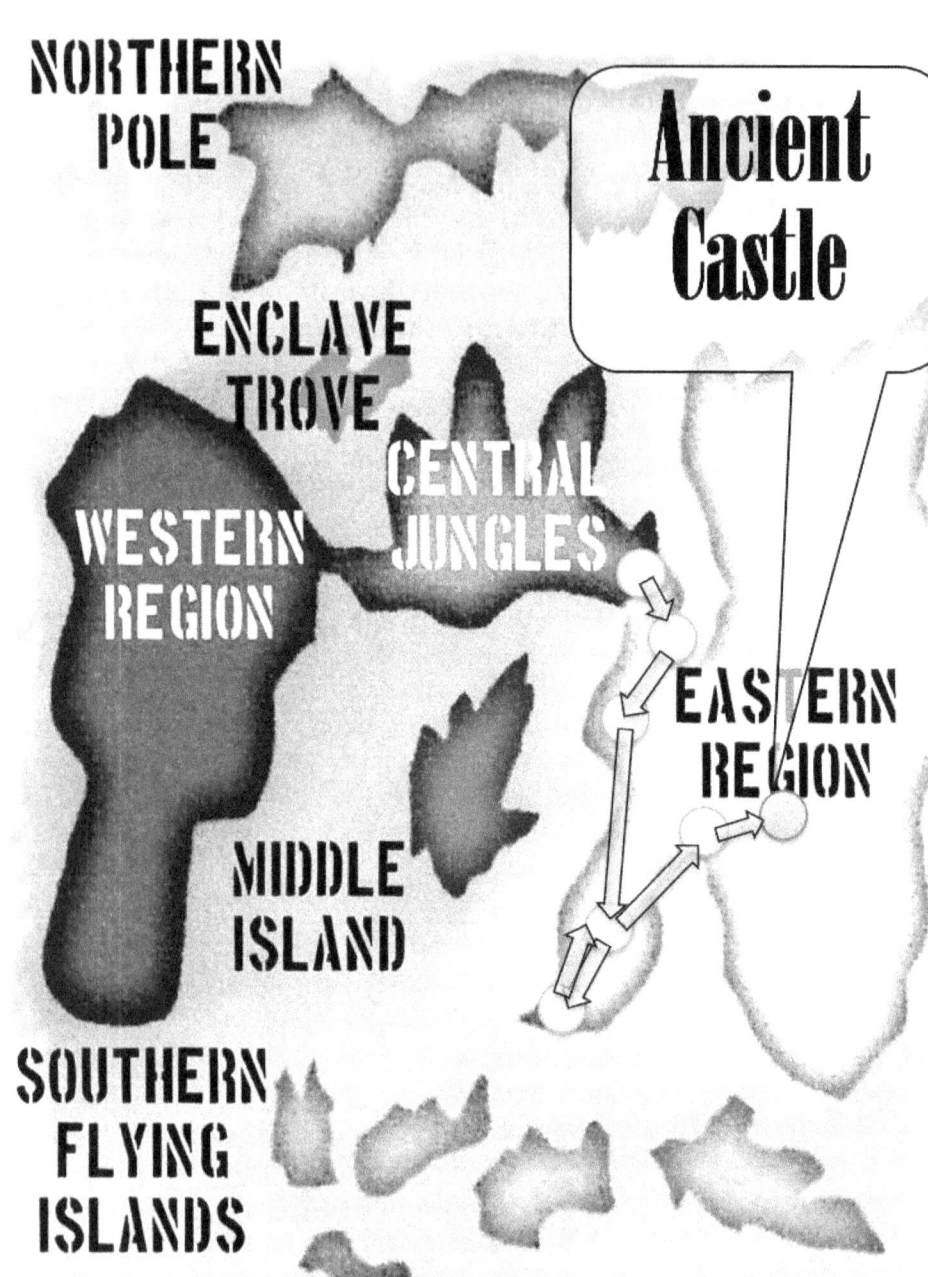

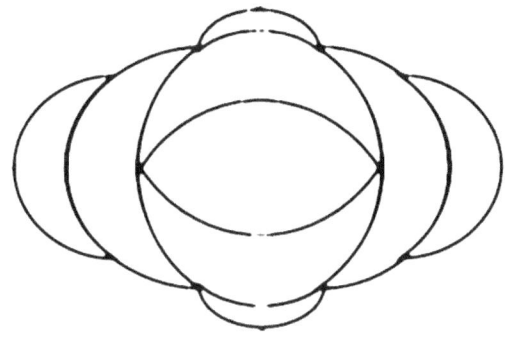

Chapter VIII: Obayifo

Primeval buildings from fifty-thousand years ago were scattered about the land; Enlightened have survived this whole time, but people have come and gone throughout this long period of time.

Reaching a castle from this old period, the group finally decided to stop for the night. It had already been almost a full day since they left Amaya's city.

"This looks like a wonderful place to stop." Hideaki said.

"Seriously?" Skye asked, "It's a creepy castle from thousands of years ago..."

"And I'm a creepy man from thousands of years ago!" Hideaki said.

"Right..." Skye said.

Hideaki chuckled as he led them to the creepy castle. Volf stayed silent in fear of the terrible monsters that he seems to think might be around every corner.

"Hello?" Hideaki shouted at the castle's front gate, "Is anyone here?"

There was no response from the bastion now overgrown with vines and trees.

"Well," Volf said, "nobody's home. Let's leave!"

"I agree!" Skye said, "It's really scary here and I just don't want to be here."

"Skye," Hideaki said, "I am talking to one of the Keys to the Vault of Four Moons that's inside of the castle. We can't leave until we get it."

"What kind of horror play is this that I'm in?!" Skye said.

"Play?" Hideaki asked, "What nonsense. Let's go inside! Universal—"

"Let's not!" Skye interrupted, "I know there's a key in there, but—"

"There is nothing we can do about the creepiness here, Skye." Hideaki said, "We have to go inside. Chaos!"

Two separated words seemed to be enough to summon Hideaki's powers. Winds as sharp as could be slashed through the front gate and it crumbled into splinters.

"Let's go inside, I guess..." Skye said, "Where is the key, Hideaki? I can't hear it talking anywhere."

"I think these Keys may only be able to talk to one person until they're found." Hideaki said.

"That makes sense, I guess." Skye said, "Like a sort of security feature!"

"Yes," Hideaki said, "but I think that I may be wrong, as well. I think the Key is... calling for help."

"What do you mean?"

"I think someone is using its Soul energy..."

"Wait," Volf said, "don't these things have infinite Soul energy, since they're immortal?"

"Sort of." Skye said, "They still have to regenerate after a certain point. But each time they regenerate they have way more than the time they had before."

"So this one is probably being farmed for Soul energy!" Volf said.

"That may be." Hideaki said, "I think I know where it is. The top of the castle! We have to run to stop it from being used for whatever purpose."

Hideaki ran as Skye and Volf followed closely behind. They all wondered who could need such a massive amount of Soul energy.

"I can hear it screaming, now!" Skye said, "It's in a lot of pain..."

"Speaking of hearing it," Hideaki said, "have you asked the last Key we got for its name yet?"

"No." Skye said, "I think it was being used in the same way as the Key in this castle."

"Being overused?" Volf asked.

"Yes. It's asleep right now because of the terrible pain Ayé caused by using its power."

"This makes sense now." Hideaki said, "She used her power in that Key to take control of cities and put into the minds of the people deceptions, making them turn against one another. This caused anarchy in those cities once they left them leaderless."

"Wait," Skye said, "doesn't that mean that Kione probably had another one of the Keys, too?"

"Of course!" Hideaki said, "That is the reason they were married. They are very alike, indeed. They probably mesmerized each other with their powers and caused one another to fall in love."

"Does that mean they really are in love then?" Volf asked.

"No!" Skye said, "You're such an idiot..."

"Actually," Hideaki said, "he's right. Love caused by Soul energy is true love."

"Oh..." Skye said while Volf just smiled at his small victory.

"Nonetheless," Hideaki said, "this means that we need to go after those two again. We need that other Key."

"How is it that they control the energy in the Keys, Hideaki?" Skye asked.

"It must be that staff Ayé uses." Hideaki said.

"How do you know that?" Volf asked.

"It is something I should have told you about when I told you of the Orb of Night." Hideaki said, "But we have no time now. There's the exit to the roof!"

Outside they saw Usha dancing around a fire in the darkness just as it began to rain. She looked to be doing some strange ritual.

"There's the key!" Volf said.

"Where?" Skye asked.

"In the fire pit!"

"Usha!" Hideaki yelled, "Give us that orb!"

"Too late." Usha said, "Obayifo, use this source of almost limitless energy to open your portal to this world! Help me Dark Saint!"

"Take the key!" Skye yelled.

"Universal Chaos!" Hideaki shouted and a tornado came forth and put out the fire in the fire pit.

"I've already taken the Soul energy I need for the ritual." Usha said, "Run, because a Dark Saint more powerful than me is coming to kill you."

Hideaki grabbed the key from the ashes.

"Run, you two!" he shouted.

Volf and Skye ran downward as Hideaki lagged slightly behind.

"It feels like fire burning me." the Key said in a young boy's voice, "I'm still only twelve. I didn't know giving up my body would allow me to feel pain. It's like being in the Realm of the Demons!"

"Don't cry, boy." Hideaki said, "You're safe, now. We've rescued you. Go to sleep."

"Okay..." the boy said in a painful voice.

"Usha will pay for this..." Hideaki thought.

Back on the roof, Usha watched as Obayifo appeared from lightning out of the sky and struck right next to Usha.

"Obayifo!" Usha said excitingly.

"Usha." Obayifo said.

"Is that all you have to say?" she asked.

"Is that all you have to say, Usha? I greeted you in the same manner as you did for me."

"Right, sorry Obayifo." she said.

"Remember," Obayifo said, "you don't have to treat me like a master. You are your own goddess. You are powerful and you can do whatever you want – just like me."

"Of course, Obayifo." she said, "Would you like to help me kill some stupid kids and an old man that tried to stop me from opening your portal?"

"Sure, Usha." he said in a plain and lifeless voice.

Obayifo ran downstairs quickly, leaving Usha behind.

"Why did I ever open that portal?" she asked herself, "He's right... I am a goddess. I could have killed them myself!"

Nearing the front gate, the group could hear Obayifo chasing after them.

"You two!" Hideaki shouted while handing Skye the Key, "If Obayifo reaches us then you need to get out of here. I will hold this monstrosity here as long as possible."

"We can't do that to you, Hideaki!" Skye shouted.

"Yeah!" Volf said, "What could we even do without you? We aren't strong enough, yet. And we don't even know where to begin looking for the other Key!"

"You will just have to deal with that and–"

"And what?" Obayifo said from behind Hideaki.

Hideaki turned around as Skye and Volf backed away slowly.

"Leave, you two!" Hideaki yelled, "You can't stay here!"

"We can't leave you!" Skye said with tears in her eyes.

"Please don't do this to us..." Volf said with a red face as he held back his own tears.

"It's fine..." Hideaki said with a face full of tears, "Leave me here and survive. I gave up my immortality to protect people like you two. Get my mother to help you, she'll—"

"No!" Skye shouted, "We want to travel with you! Not that super young looking old lady!"

"Please, Hideaki!" Volf said, "Let's run, now!"

"Leave them alone!" Usha shouted as she jumped down the steps onto Obayifo.

"What are you doing, Usha?!" he asked.

"I'm sending you back!" she shouted, "Cosmic Reverse!"

Obayifo turned into lightning and he shot through a nearby window and into the sky once more.

"Usha..." Hideaki said softly, "Usha! Why did you help us?"

"I didn't." she said, "I'm just going to kill you myself!"

"No you won't!" Volf yelled, "Universal Chaos!"

Winds shot from Volf quickly pushed Usha back to the top of the nearby steps and into the wall. She was pinned.

Skye's tattoo began to glow brightly and it came forth from her forehead and formed a Staff with a Heart at its end, like it did once before.

"Universal Complete Annihilation." she said with her staff pointed at Usha.

"You can't kill an immortal being!" Usha shouted, "But I can kill you! Universal Complete Annihilation!"

A dark beam of energy shot from Usha's fingertip as a dark energy gathered around Skye's staff and shot at Usha. The beams collided and stopped Volf's winds that had pinned Usha.

"What's happening?" Usha asked with a scared looking face.

"The two beams make up too much Cosmic energy! It'll destroy the whole castle!" Hideaki shouted, "Run!"

Skye's staff imprinted back into her forehead and went dark again.

The three of them began to run, but Usha was trapped on the other side of the castle with the energy building up in the center and about to blow.

After spiraling for just a few seconds the blasts finally built up too much energy in the castle and it began to expand into a Planet Crumbler power.

"If the planet dies then not even immortal beings will survive..." Usha said, "Planet Crumbler!"

She created her own Planet Crumbler and sent it at the expanding and far more powerful one in the center of the room.

At the collision – the Planet Crumbler began to expand at a much greater rate than before. It was the shape of a huge sphere that just would not stop getting bigger. It consumed anything it touched and kept going.

"A Planet Crumbler!" Hideaki said, "Grab my hands!"

Skye took his right hand and Volf took his other.

"I hope this works." Hideaki said, "I'm going to use Nazar's power. Icy Grave!"

A nearby pond gushed up from the ground and surrounded them; it froze and formed the impenetrable shield that they needed.

The Planet Crumbler reached them and pushed them for many kilometers to the south before it finally exploded into an explosion bigger than that of a hydrogen bomb.

Much of the central part of the Eastern region was decimated in this blast; the group landed near the Southern Harbor.

Hatching from the ice the group was fine, but very shaken up.

"Are you two okay?" Hideaki asked.

"I'm fine." Skye said holding onto her head that she seemed to have bumped.

"Me too…" Volf said, "I cut my hand, though."

"Let me see it, Volf." Hideaki said.

"Body Undoing!" He shouted and a green light surrounded the cut and almost instantaneously healed it.

"What now?" Skye asked.

"Now," Hideaki said, "We head to Southern Harbor."

"What's there?" Volf asked.

"It's the only way to Middle Island. I just hope that we can also find Kione and Ayé there."

"It's probably the only city left for them to take over." Skye said, "I'm sure they're there."

"I agree." Hideaki said, "Do you need healing for you head, Skye?"

"Sure."

"Body Undoing!" he said and a green light dropped to her forehead

As the light hit her forehead Skye's tattoo lit up and it pushed the green light away from her head.

"Seriously?" Skye said, "Please, let him heal me..."

"Body Undoing!" he repeated and more green light seeped onto her forehead.

This time as it hit her head the same thing happened.

"I think it's afraid you're trying to get rid of it..." Skye said, "I guess I'll just have to deal with the headache from bumping my head."

"Very well..." Hideaki said, "Let's go."

Off they went to the nearby south; they were so close to the Southern Harbor that they could feel the salt in the sea winds.

Not sleeping for almost two days they were very tired and ready to find a great place to sleep or any place to sleep at all.

NORTHERN POLE

Southern Harbor

ENCLAVE TROVE

CENTRAL JUNGLES

WESTERN REGION

EASTERN REGION

MIDDLE ISLAND

SOUTHERN FLYING ISLANDS

Sphere Zero

Chapter IX: Staff of Night

Just as they had assumed – when they reached the Southern Harbor, they found the town had a sign declaring anarchy within. Kione and Ayé were in control.

Noises came from within the city walls. Screams and cries, explosions and fires, pets and whatever else could be heard.

"Inside the town," Hideaki said, "don't speak to anyone. There is no law inside. We won't be safe until we board a ship to Middle Island."

"But we still have to get the Key from Kione and Ayé before we leave." Skye said.

"That's correct." Hideaki said, "I'm sure that we'll find them somewhere at a high vantage point from which they can watch the chaos inside the city."

"There's a lighthouse at the pier." Volf said, "It looks like it, anyway."

"You're right, idiot!" Skye said.

"Then how am I an idiot?"

"Oh, sorry." Skye said, "I don't even notice when I say it anymore."

"Anyway," Hideaki said, "let's go to that lighthouse. I think Volf was right about it."

They walked into the town and they saw that the streets were in chaos. Outside the walls they had heard the horror but now they had to see it with their own eyes.

Dead bodies littered the streets; children were left without parents as they sat on the streets alone, pets had no owners and ran around in packs in the city.

Anarchy was in full effect.

"How did Kione and Ayé take this town so quickly?!" Skye asked.

"Southern Harbor never had an official government." Hideaki said, "The people simply followed whoever was strongest. Most of the time it was pirates or mercenary gangs that had power. Unfortunately it's now Leyb's disgusting generals."

"What should we do?" Volf asked.

"We're here to stop Kione and Ayé." Hideaki said, "So let's do it. Then I'll pay some local mercenaries or pirates to take control."

"Maybe we should have them take control before we stop them?" Skye suggested.

"People are dying…" Hideaki said, "Yes, we'll hire some people to take control first. I know a large tavern here where we can hire thousands of mercenaries."

"Do you have enough money for that, Hideaki?" Skye asked.

"I do." Hideaki said, "Sixty-two thousand years is enough time to gather a lot of money."

"Good point." Skye said.

Hideaki led the group through the dangerous town. They ran into a few different groups trying to mug them, but Hideaki defended them with his Universal Chaos power as needed. No real trouble crossed them.

"Here we are." Hideaki said.

"Southern Harbor Tavern." Skye said, "These people are really creative…"

"Yeah…" Volf said, "Southern Harbor – a harbor in the south. Southern Harbor Tavern – a tavern at the southern harbor…"

Inside of the huge tavern a group of Leyb's soldiers were fighting the local thugs.

"Hey!" a soldier yelled, "This is our town now. Kione and Ayé demand it!"

"Kione and Ayé declared anarchy." Hideaki interrupted, "I'm sure that anarchy means that no one is in charge, now."

"Stupid old man!" the soldier yelled, "Let's kill him first!"

"Killing an old man?" a pirate yelled, "Not even we'd do that!"

The pirate drew his knife and slit the soldier's throat. Five soldiers that followed him in decided to make a run for their lives.

"Good job!" Hideaki said, "I'm willing to pay any group that will make order in this town."

"How much?" the pirate asked.

"Ten-thousand gold coins per person."

"I'll tell my boss right now!" the pirate said.

"I heard him." A man said from the corner of the room, "We'll take the offer, Hideaki."

"My old friend!" Hideaki shouted, "How are you, Sutton?"

"I'm fine, friend." Sutton said, "Who are these two friends of yours?"

"The young woman is Skye and the young man is Volf."

"It's nice to meet you two, Skye and Volf." Sutton said.

"Nice to meet you too, Sutton." Skye said.

"Yeah!"

"Is that all you can say, Volf?" Skye asked.

"Well I said yeah to agree with what you said..."

"Never mind, Volf."

"Did you only come to this town to make order, Hideaki?" Sutton asked, "Or is there a goal you're after, like usual?"

"The usual." Hideaki said, "I'm here to take a magical staff and a magical orb from Kione and Ayé."

"I tried to fight them off." Sutton said, "They were very powerful when using that thing. It was almost like they tried to control my mind with it…"

"The orb is a source of infinite Soul energy when used in terrible ways." Hideaki said, "These orbs used to be Enlightened. They gave up their souls to become Keys – keys to a vault on Middle Island where four of the pieces of the Orb of Night are hidden."

"So, you're gathering the Orb of Night. Is that to stop Leyb?"

"Yes, Sutton." Hideaki said, "Now, you said that you chose to fight off Kione and Ayé. Does that mean you've lost your immortality?"

"Yes, Hideaki. But two-thousand years is enough for me, anyhow. I'll do what I need to do to maintain some order in this town if you promise to stop those two."

"Very well." Hideaki said.

"So, you must have lost your immortality, too. You're fighting against Leyb."

"That is correct." Hideaki said.

"Well, then. I respect you infinitely more now, Hideaki."

"And I respect you the same, Sutton. I hope that your years you have left will allow you to wrap your life up."

"I've already wrapped up everything I need to, Hideaki. Now, I need that money to pay the guys to help me make order. Do you have it with you?"

"Yes, I carry only one-hundred thousand gold coins with me, though. Go to my old hideout in Enclave Trove and get my hidden riches. They're all yours, now."

"Ah, one last journey before I settle down! I'll just pay the soldiers what I can with this one-hundred thousand for now and get that money later. I can't go all the way around the continents right now just to pick up some money."

"We're off, then." Hideaki said.

Hideaki led Skye and Volf out of the tavern and Sutton sent his people out into the town and they began to stop fights – kill, capture and scare off Leyb's soldiers – and simply act like a regular police force. Sutton was a very good man to most people of the town and many followed him for free.

"Now," Skye said, "what's the magical staff that Ayé has, Hideaki?"

"It's the control staff for the Orb of Night." Hideaki said, "It's the only way to recombine the pieces and make sure that we can control it when it is whole."

"Why didn't you just tell us about it before?" Volf asked.

"I wasn't wanting you two to know that the power was so powerful that it had to be controlled with a staff..."

"I see." Skye said, "Only dangerous powers are controlled with magical staves. Right?"

"Yes, Skye." Hideaki said, "Now, let's go get that staff and the final Key."

They marched to the pier and straight to the lighthouse. There was a single door that was propped open.

"It looks like someone else broke in already." Hideaki said.

"Maybe it's Sutton's people?" Skye suggested.

"No." Hideaki said, "I think it is Usha."

"Why do you think that?" Volf asked.

"She was following us on our short way here; she was stalking us. Now she's just trying to eliminate two people she thinks might be able to hurt us."

"Kione and Ayé..." Skye said.

"Should we help them?" Volf asked.

"Yes." Hideaki said, "I think those two just need to be shown love by other people. That is why they do these raids on cities – they don't understand that others can be just like the both of them. I think the Keys may have deformed their minds in some way."

"Yeah," Skye said, "a person could have major problems when they're exposed to another person's Soul energy for too long."

"Did your tattoo tell you that, Skye?" Hideaki asked.

"No," Skye said, "it was Yoko. She told me a lot of stuff before she went to sleep when we found her in Yoichi's dojo caverns."

"Anyway, "Hideaki said, "are you two ready to help Kione and Ayé against Usha?"

"Yeah!" Volf said.

"Definitely."

" Good. Usha is a disgusting and evil person – she kills people in horrible ways."

Hideaki guided the others up the stairs – not that there was much guiding needed to go up a spiral staircase with no side-paths.

After moments of walking they reached the door to the top; Usha was outside in front of Kione and Ayé, pretending to be friendly to them.

"Usha, we just don't want you in our town." Ayé said, "Leyb gave you your own army. Go have fun attacking your own towns with them."

"Ayé!" Usha yelled, "Aren't you listening? They're all dead! Never mind. Universal Complete Annihilation!"

A beam of energy shot from Usha's fingertip directly at Ayé, but Ayé simply blocked it with her Key.

"You can't kill this Key." Ayé said, "These things used to be Enlightened. They've given up their bodies for immortality that can't be taken from them. Your Universal Complete Annihilation attack is useless."

"So that's what those are..." Usha said, "All well. I'll just suck your Soul energy until you die!"

"Planet Crumbler!" Ayé said with her staff pointed at Usha.

A large ball of plasma – hotter than the sun – shot directly at Usha and pushed her backward.

"I survived a much more potent version of this attack!" Usha said.

"Probably at night." Kione taunted, "It's not your lucky day."

"Universal Crumbler!" Usha shouted.

Ayé's Planet Crumbler then turned dark blue like a blue dwarf star and shot back at Kione and Ayé.

"What is this attack?!" Kione asked, "Give me the staff, Ayé!"

Kione took the staff and pointed it at the big ball of incredibly hot plasma.

"Universal Complete Annihilation!" he shouted.

Exploiting the Key's last bit of Soul energy, Kione blasted the Universal Crumbler and it imploded.

The resulting blast pulled in Usha as she screamed. The imploded sphere just kept pulling in everything in the surrounding and the lighthouse began to bend inward.

"Kione and Ayé!" Hideaki shouted, "You need to get down here! You'll die!"

"Why do you care?!" Ayé asked angrily.

"I care about every human on our planet. I care about all living things. Your minds have been corrupted by that Key you carry. It slowly degrades your mind and makes you go insane. You don't really believe we hate you – your mind has just degraded over time. You need to let the staff and the orb go."

"Ayé..." Kione said, "I think he's right. I've been without my orb since that night in the town we first met these people. I've been thinking that what we're doing may be wrong... We should give them the staff."

"Okay, Kione." Ayé said as she looked at Kione and tossed the staff at Hideaki, "Here! You'd better be right! Usha will be after us and we won't have a way to defend ourselves!"

"I am right!" Hideaki shouted to overpower the strong winds of the imploded sphere.

Skye caught the staff just as it was about to be sucked up by the strong winds. Kione and Ayé turned around and got into a strange basket.

"Where are you going?!" Hideaki asked.

"To the skies!" Ayé said as a huge balloon appeared above her head from behind the light of the lighthouse, "It's a hot air balloon! Kione and I invented it!"

"Wow…" Volf said.

"Idiot! We don't have time for this, let's go!"

"Right, sorry Skye.

Hideaki led the group down the steps as quickly as he could. Skye tried to hold onto the staff and Key as best she could.

Reaching the bottom, Sutton was waiting for the group to arrive.

"What happened up there?!" he shouted.

"Kione and Ayé weren't such bad people." Skye said, "They just needed what we all need. People who care."

"Seriously?" Sutton asked, "Well, whatever happened. We need to get out of here! That thing will suck us up if we don't get away from here!"

Lighting the pier for the last time, the lighthouse was sucked up into the sphere as the group ran for their lives.

Once they reached town, the sphere finally exploded and debris flew in all directions. The pier was decimated by the explosion and debris.

Ships sank and buildings caught fire. People were injured and many died in the blast.

"What caused that?" Sutton asked.

"It was Usha." Hideaki said, "She's a v−"

"I know what she is." Sutton said, "Leyb's General!"

"Not just that, she's a−"

"There's no time to talk, now." Sutton said, "You need to get on my ship. I got my men to send for a small boat to bring you out to my ship in the bay."

"Aren't you coming, Sutton?" Skye asked.

"No." Sutton responded, "My men are going to drop you off on Middle Island and then come back for me once I've secured this town fully. Then we're off to get you guys and drop you off near the Central Jungle to Eastern Region border. Now, get on the boat before Usha's soldiers get here! There are hundreds of them right behind me!"

"Run!" Hideaki yelled.

The group ran to the boat as it came to the docks; they jumped right onto it and they went out to sea. Just as they did, though, Usha was seen still alive and leading her army.

"Sutton!" Hideaki yelled, "Watch out for Usha! She's a vampire!"

"A what?" Sutton asked, "What's that?"

"They're immortal like Enlightened," Hideaki shouted, "but they follow the exact opposite of the Old Ones' teachings!"

"Immortal..." Sutton said to himself as the group faded into the fog of the bay.

"So," Hideaki said, "what is this Key's name, Skye?"

"This one is asleep." She said, "I don't think it's going to wake up. I think it's... angry at us for taking it from Kione and Ayé."

"It must have grown attached to them." Hideaki said, "These Keys are still humans, after all."

"Do you want the staff, Hideaki?" Skye asked.

"Yes," Hideaki said, "but we'll need my mother's Moon's Gravity Cosmic power to pull the orb and the staff apart. Or we can just take the orb to the Vault of Four Moons."

"I'm guessing we're doing the latter." Volf said.

"Do you even have to ask that, Volf?" Skye said.

"Yes, Volf does." Hideaki said, "He is an idiot, after all!"

"Seriously, enough of the idiot jokes..." Volf said.

"I'm sorry, Volf." Hideaki said, "I got caught up in the moment. But that question you asked was pretty pointless..."

"Whatever..."

"It's okay, Volf." Skye said, "I still think you're the best friend in the world – my insults to you are just the way I am."

"Thanks, Skye."

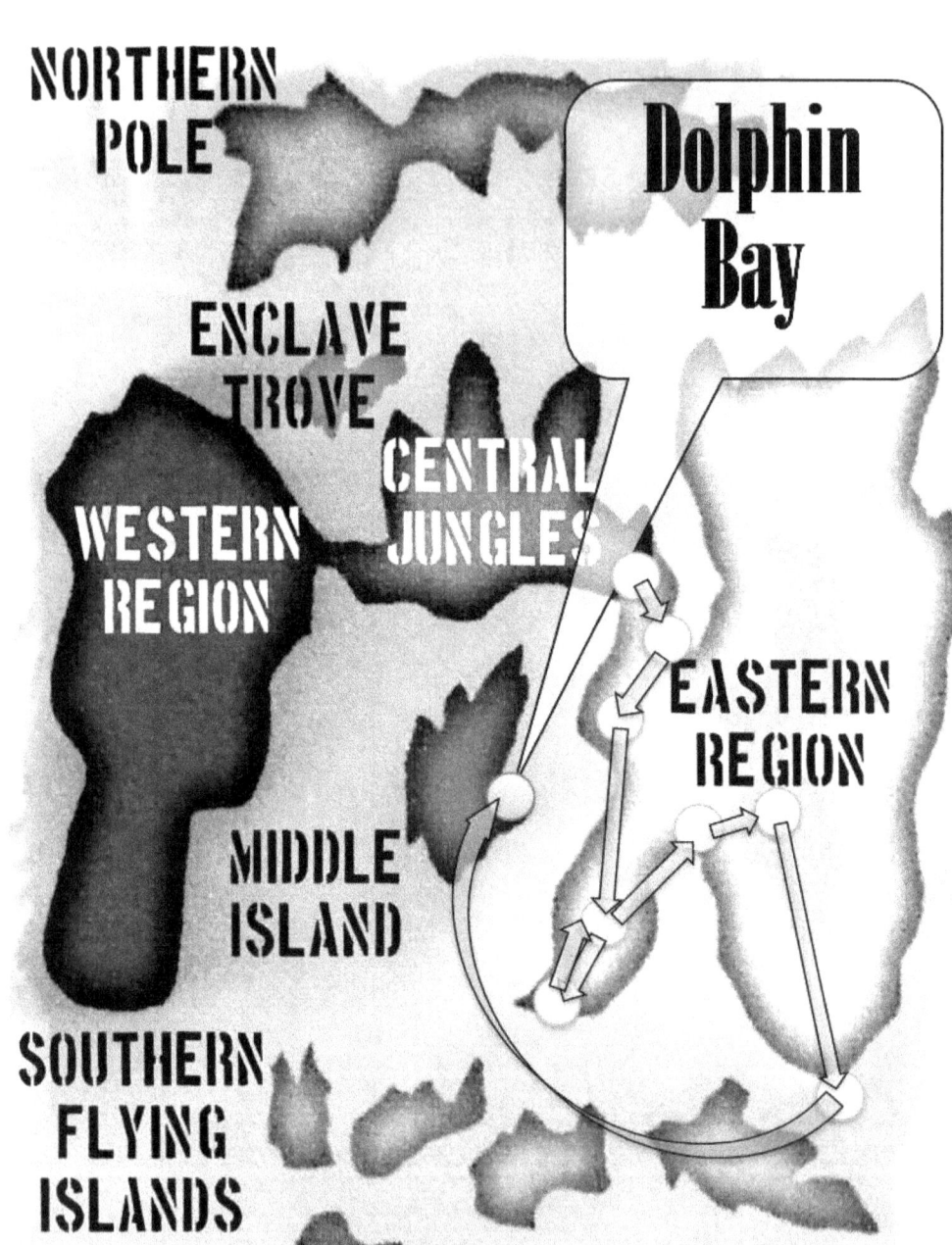

NORTHERN POLE

ENCLAVE TROVE

Dolphin Bay

CENTRAL JUNGLES

WESTERN REGION

EASTERN REGION

MIDDLE ISLAND

SOUTHERN FLYING ISLANDS

Sphere Zero

Chapter X: Elder Tribal
Stories

"Dolphin bay is the only place we can bring you from here!" the ship's first mate said, "There is a beach on the other side of Middle Island where we will come to get you in three weeks. Be ready for us."

"Will Sutton be taking us along on his trip to Enclave Trove?" Hideaki asked.

"No, old man." The first mate responded, "But he will be here when we pick you up."

"That must be a relief to you." Volf said, "Being in charge of Sutton's ship must be hard to do alone."

"Sometimes." He said, "But the seas demand a lot of us all the time, so I like the challenge."

Traveling for two weeks, the group made it to Middle Island's Dolphin Bay. Hideaki, Skye and Volf all exited the ship on a small boat and left on the island as the boat was brought back to the ship.

The group watched as the ship sailed off into the distance. Large trees, vines and many other types of plant life covered this island.

Volf and Skye walked up the cliffs from the bay and as they did they saw a magnificent view of Yoichi's dojo and his town. It looked small from such a distance, but it was still a wondrous site – even though his town was burnt down by Nazar.

"Do you know where the vault's at, Hideaki?" Volf asked.

"No. I think we should ask one of the Keys."

"Good idea." Skye said, "Yoko, are you awake?"

"Yes, Skye."

"Can you tell us where to go to find the Vault of Four Moons?"

"It's at the northern tip of Middle Island." Yoko said, "Just head northward and you'll eventually see it at the very top of the highest of cliffs."

"How long will it take us to travel there?" Hideaki asked.

"About one week." She responded, "And you will want to head west from there to reach Jungle Escape Bay, where your friends will be coming with their ship in three weeks."

"How long from the vault to Jungle Escape?" Hideaki asked.

"About five days. You will probably need to wait for over a week before your friends arrive for you. They said they would be back three weeks from today. Is that all you have to ask? I wish to sleep now."

"One more question." Hideaki said, "What do we do with the Keys when we arrive at the Vault of Four Moons?"

"Simply place us into the slots on the vault door and it will open. It's alien technology which we will power with our Soul energy."

"Very well..." Hideaki said, "We have no more questions. You may sleep."

"Goodnight, Yoko." Skye said.

"Goodnight, everyone." Yoko responded.

Hideaki led the group through the jungle for miles and they rested only every few hours. Each day seemed like an eternity in the jungles of Middle Island.

"Middle Island was once part of a far bigger Central Region." Hideaki told them as they hiked, "It was ruined long ago in a terrible war. Now the only parts left of the Central Region are the Central Jungles and Middle Island. The rest sank into the ocean."

"I've heard that story, before." Skye said, "That's what happened to Shangrat-Lantis, right?"

"Yes." Hideaki said, "The fabled city of death. Shangrat-Lantis was lost long ago in the war and no one has seen even a trace of it since then."

"Did you ever see it, Hideaki?"

"No, Volf. Unfortunately, few people ever found the hidden city. It was somewhere in the Central Region where I never had the chance to explore before its destruction."

"How long ago was it when all that happened?" Skye asked.

"About fifty-thousand years ago. It was the war that happened just before our last fifty-thousand year era of peace – which just now ended with Leyb."

"And now the Eastern Region already suffered a huge blow to Leyb's armies." Skye said.

"Yes, and I'm afraid that he'll destroy the entire Eastern Region if we don't stop him soon. Usha caused a huge blast to destroy the center of our continent, and now we have to stop him before he destroys everything else like the Central Region was destroyed long ago."

"What kind of weapon could have caused an entire continent to be destroyed, though?" Skye asked.

"The Orb of Night." Hideaki said, "But don't worry, it won't cause that destruction as long as we only use it a few times."

"Is it really that powerful?" Volf asked.

"Yes. We have to be very careful to use it only when we need it and then separate the Orb of Night once again."

Volf and Skye then looked at each other with a bit of fear in their eyes.

"Should we just try to stop Leyb without the Orb of Night?" Skye asked.

"Yeah," Volf said, "I don't think I want to accidentally destroy our entire continent..."

"It's fine." Hideaki said, "There are clear rules on the usage of the Orb of Night, just like there are on being Enlightened or being a Vampire. I won't let it happen."

"If you say so, Hideaki..." Skye mumbled.

Days and days of traveling took a lot out of the group; they had to forage for berries and hunt for their own food as needed.

They came across a few small villages of people who were all very good people; they treated the group to meals and even their tribal customs like dancing, storytelling and other rituals.

"This planet used to have many languages." The storyteller said, "After the war fifty-thousand years ago the entire world converted to only one language so we could all get along together. Sadly, there are still people in our world that will not get along and seek to harm everyone else; to take their land, their belongings, their lives and their freedom."

The storyteller told many stories of the ancient past; ancient past according to them, anyway – Hideaki told about how he was Enlightened and that he lived for sixty-two thousand years and the people of these villages respected him in his storytelling.

Finally, the group set off on their seventh day of travels and they could already see the Vault of Four Moons.

It had been about seven weeks and four days since the war with Leyb had begun. They were almost at the final stretch in their journey.

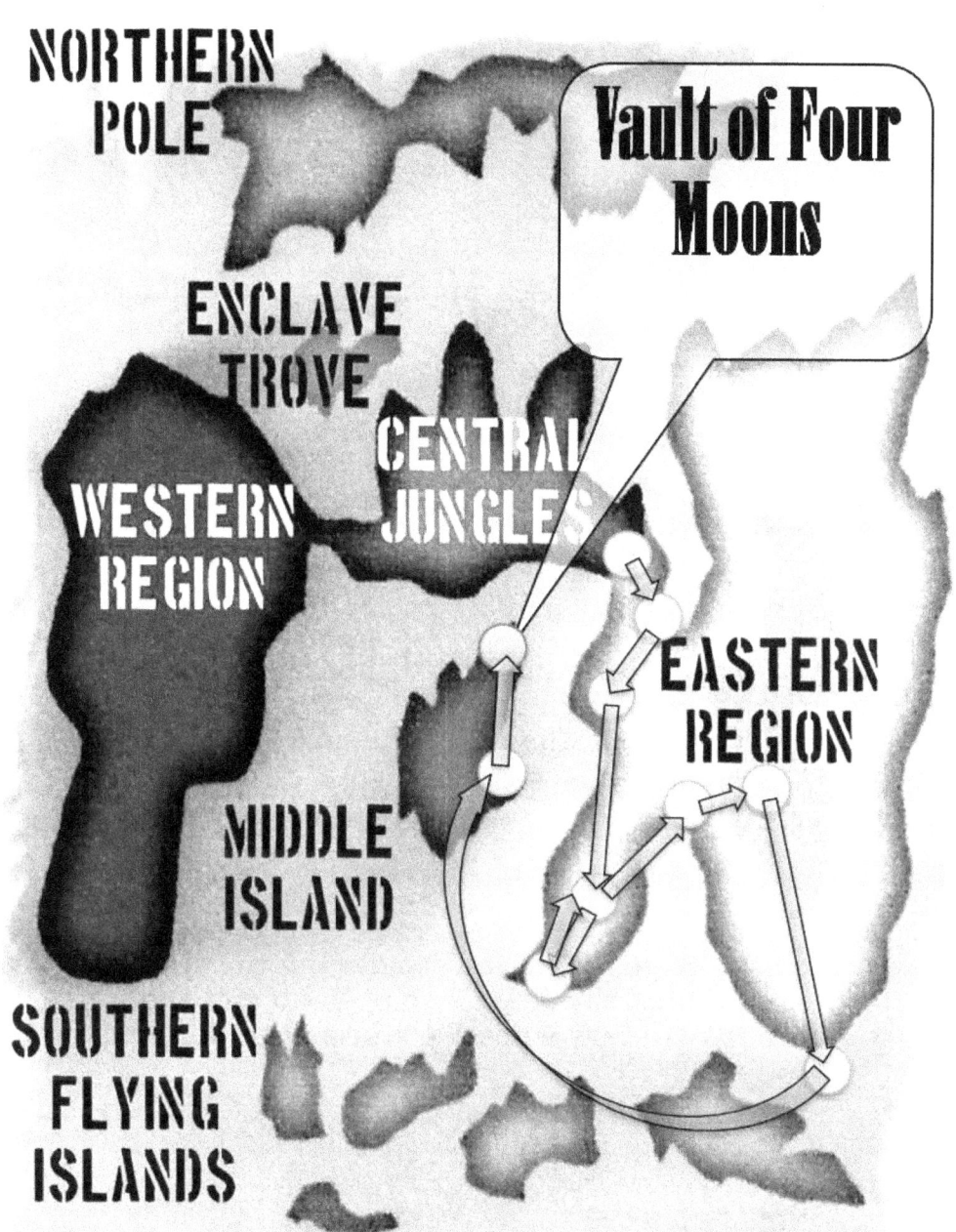

NORTHERN POLE

ENCLAVE TROVE

Vault of Four Moons

CENTRAL JUNGLES

WESTERN REGION

EASTERN REGION

MIDDLE ISLAND

SOUTHERN FLYING ISLANDS

Sphere Zero

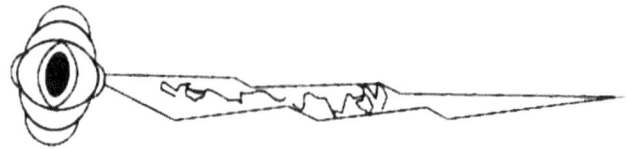

Chapter XI: Vault of Four Moons

Reaching the top of the cliff, they saw the strange alien doorway with the four slots on it that Yoko had told them about.

"Finally." Hideaki said.

"Yeah, I'm tired of holding Yoko and the other Keys... they're starting to get heavy!"

"Skye, you're only carrying the staff with one of the Keys. I took Yoko and the other two Keys when we stopped in the first village..."

"Idiot!" Skye said, "Don't you know not to correct me by now, Volf!"

"Right..."

"Sutton isn't coming for two weeks." Hideaki said, "I guess I can allow you two to argue until that day, so we can waste more time... But I'd rather we get the four pieces before Leyb takes over the entire Eastern Region."

"Okay," Skye said, "Yoko, I'm placing you into the door."

"Goodbye, Skye."

"What do you mean, Yoko?"

"Once we are all placed into the door, we will be absorbed fully. The door will unlock and you will take the pieces of the Orb of Night and leave. Then, the vault will shut – and we Keys will be trapped inside the invincible doors forever."

"We can't do that to you!" Skye said.

"You can." Yoko said, "It's what we four chose a long time ago. We four Keys knew each other well before we became such; we will have all four of us forever to keep each other company."

"Do it, Skye." Volf said, "I know it's hard for you to let a good friend go, but you have to. I'll be here for you."

"Okay…" Skye said, "Goodbye, Yoko. You are a very, very good friend."

"Thank you, Skye." Yoko said, "And I'll miss you too, idiot."

"Hey!" Volf shouted, "Is that all you will remember me as?"

"No, I'll remember a brave young man that saved Skye's life when Leyb attacked the City of Customs."

"Thanks, Yoko. I'll remember how awesome you were, forever."

"Goodbye, Yoko." Hideaki said, "It was great to travel with another Enlightened like myself."

"I respect you, Hideaki. The other Keys will never forget how you led Volf and Skye to rescuing them. I will never forget."

Skye then pointed the Staff with a Key at one of the four slots on the vault door and it attached. Volf then placed the other three orbs onto the door.

When Volf placed the final one, the attached staff fell to the ground and the Keys disappeared into the door. Their Soul energy was sucked inside and the vault door opened.

"I'll miss you, Yoko..." Skye thought.

"Down the steps, then." Hideaki said.

They walked down a few miles of steps and they came into an underground palace of sorts.

"This is the same place that was below Yoichi's dojo!" Skye shouted.

"You're right..." Hideaki said, "I knew it looked to stretch for an eternity, but I think now that these underground passages might travel throughout the entire world..."

"Wow!" Volf whispered in a fascinated voice.

"It may be the same area," Hideaki said, "but this one is shielded by Soul energy.

There would be no way to access this spot from the surrounding areas."

"So maybe the entire world isn't open." Skye said, "Even if it is all attached by this place."

"No," Hideaki said, "I think that this is the only place protected by such a magic."

"There're the four pieces!" Volf shouted as he pointed at a nearby pillar that reached up into darkness.

"I see." Hideaki said, "So the pieces were put on display for anyone outside of the shield to see, but they could never really get into this place even if they saw it."

Volf ran and grabbed the four pieces from the display on the wall.

"Here are four of the pieces of the ultimate weapon: the Orb of Night." A sign read above the pieces.

"Let's go." Skye said, "I'd rather not get locked into an invincible and eternal shield..."

Hideaki led the group up the steps and they walked outside of the vault.

"Vault of Four Moons – Shutting Down." Said a strange and static-laced voice from the door.

The Vault of Four Moons shut itself closed.

"I guess that voice was part of the alien technology..." Hideaki said, "I am surprised that the door can talk."

"That's kind of scary..." Volf said.

"Idiot!" Skye shouted, "Shouldn't you at least try to act tough?"

"Nah." Volf said, "There's no reason to."

"I guess not..." Skye said, "They'll already know you're a weak idiot when they see you..."

"Come on, you two." Hideaki said, "We have a bit of a ways to go to get to Jungle Escape Bay. We'll be safer when we get there."

"What do you mean, 'safer'?"

"Usha followed us here." Hideaki said, "Some of the villagers told me about something hunting their children after we arrived... Whatever it was killed them."

"It could have just been a wild animal." Skye said, "I'm sure there are a bunch in the–"

"No, Skye. It was Usha. She hunted children and killed them before she ever joined Leyb. It's no coincidence that it would start right after we stopped in their village."

"I guess it's a good thing." Volf said, "At least we can take the last piece of the Orb of Night, now."

"Yeah, idiot." Skye said, "But how are we going to beat her if we find her? She'll probably attack at night."

"There's no problem." Hideaki said, "The Orb of Night can kill Enlightened, so I'm sure it could kill a Vampire as well."

"This Orb of Night is just sounding more horrible each time." Skye said, "First it can destroy continents and second it can kill immortal people?!"

"Aether energy is what it's called." Hideaki said, "Aether energy is the only energy known to harm an immortal being. The only way known to use such energy is the Orb of Night."

"Whatever, Hideaki." Skye said, "If you believe it's right to use the Orb of Night to kill her, then I trust you."

"It's never right to kill." Hideaki said, "But sometimes it's necessary to preserve other lives and sometimes to end a war. I would never harm an innocent, though; only those guilty of crimes like her."

"Let's go, then." Volf said, "I don't want to just stand around until nighttime. Let's get to the beach so we'll be safer."

"How is it we'll be safer at the beach, exactly?" Skye asked.

"Yeah, good point." Volf said, "I was just repeating what Hideaki said a minute ago..."

"I can use Nazar's Icy Grave Cosmic power to create an invincible shield around us until day breaks, but I need enough water to shield against her. She has the Universal Complete Annihilation attack."

"Will that shield hold against that?" Skye asked.

"I hope so!" Hideaki asked, "Otherwise, we'll just have to pilfer that last piece of the Orb of Night from her and use the complete thing to blast her into dust!"

Leaving the safety of the cliffs near the Vault of Four Moons, the group ventured into the deep jungle of the island.

Daylight stayed for hours after this time, but night always has to come eventually.

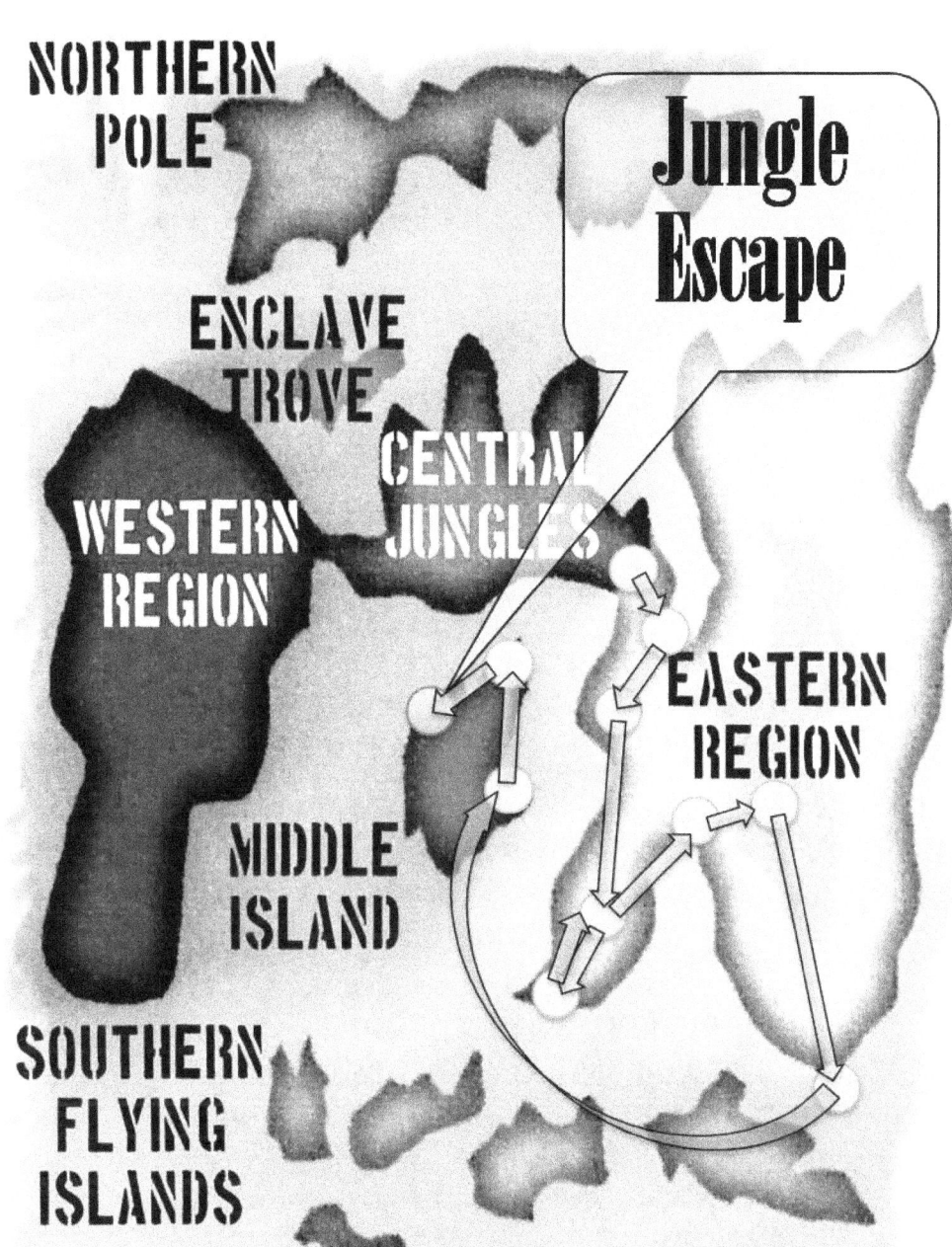

Chapter XII: Fall of a Goddess

Usha was hunting the group as soon as they arrived on Middle Island. Walking through an unknown area like this wasn't helping their chances of survival against this cunning huntress.

"I need to know where those three went!" Usha yelled to a villager, "Where are they from here?! I know they told you!"

"The Vault of Four Moons." The man's wife told her.

"And you expect me to just know where that is, woman?!" Usha asked, "Where do I go from here?"

"Go to the north of the island. It's on top of the highest cliff."

"Fine. But before I go... Universal Complete Annihilation!"

Usha's beam struck the man's wife and she turned to ash in the wind.

"No!" the man cried, "Bring her back! Please... Don't let her die..."

"She's already dead." Usha told him.

The villager fell to his knees in defeat; he felt as if his life was over.

"I'll leave you alive. I think that's more torture than anything, now that your friends and family are all dead."

"No, please!" the man cried, "At least send me to my wife! You owe me that much!"

"I'm showing you mercy. I suggest you take it. Any death I give you will be slow and painful."

"Why would you do this to us?"

"I love to see people in pain."

"But why?! How could you kill them? My wife, my friends... the children even. Couldn't you have spared them, at least?"

"Children are my absolute favorite to kill. They're so small and show the most fear. They scream and cry when I cut them to pieces and–"

"No more!" the man begged, "I don't want to hear more about what you did to them... Those poor children... You're a fiend! A Demon!

"Have a wonderful and lonely life." Usha said, "I know I have."

"You'll need a friend's help someday, Demon!" he shouted, "When you do, you're friends will abandon you like you abandoned everyone else!"

"I'm immortal." Usha alleged, "I only need the Vampire code to survive forever."

"I know about Vampires." the man said, "I also know why you're doing this now. Vampires are forced to kill and torture or they will lose their immortality. When a vampire slips up on a single rule they won't just turn into a regular person again, they'll die. You are living a very linear life, Demon. You are trapped in a cycle of death you can't escape without your own death."

Usha was angered by his knowledge and turned to kill him, but he had disappeared.

"He escaped..." Usha thought.

She looked around the area to see if he was still wandering about, but she couldn't see a trace of him – not even a footprint.

"I see!" Usha shouted, "You're Enlightened, aren't you?! You must have a Cosmic energy to make you invisible or fly or something. Well, I'll still find you once I'm done hunting those three I'm after now."

Usha turned to the north and began rushing at her quickest pace toward the Vault of Four Moons.

Upon her arrival a week later, she saw that the doors were shut.

"Strange." Usha said, "A Soul Shield Technology Portal... These are the same doors as on Obayifo's planet. SSTP AI, have you seen anyone here recently?"

"Yes." The door's computer said, "One day ago, an old man, a young man and a young woman unlocked this door with their four Keys. I then confiscated the Keys as I was instructed by the Keys."

"You don't keep many secrets, do you?"

"I am made to give any information needed to anyone to avoid any troublesome circumstances."

"Good idea." Usha said, "Now, which way did they head?"

"They headed to a place called Jungle Escape Bay to the West. They are waiting for a ship that will be arriving in thirteen days."

"Ah." Usha thought, "Good thing I took care of their pirate friend, Sutton."

"Is there anything else you wish to know?" the computer asked.

"Universal Complete Annihilation!" she shouted.

Her beam of Cosmic energy hit the door and just evaporated.

"I know nothing of the universe being completely annihilated. I am sorry for this inconvenience."

"This door is invincible!" Usha shouted, "How could you have stood against that attack?"

"I do not recall an attack." the AI said.

"Fine. I'm headed west to kill those three. I'll be back to kill you once they're dead, though!"

"I am sorry for this inconvenience, but I am not alive."

Usha screamed loudly in annoyance as she ran to the west.

Arriving at Jungle Escape Bay, Usha saw that the group had arrived before her. She silently, patiently and carefully found ambush spots over the course of a week.

She knew exactly where each of them went every day of the week and she finally decided to attack on the day before Sutton's ship was to arrive.

Skye was walking alone down a path into the woods where she was going to gather some firewood. Usha was hiding in a tree, thinking she knew exactly what to do to take Skye down.

As Skye walked under the tree, Usha jumped down and just before she landed on her, Skye's tattoo lit up and came forth from her head. It became a staff once more. It formed a shield around Skye.

Usha landed on the shield and slid off the side of it.

"What is this energy?!" Usha asked, "This doesn't feel like Cosmic energy…"

"It's not." Skye said, "It's far more powerful."

"It isn't Soul energy, either..." Usha thought to herself.

"Stumped?" Skye asked, "It's a type of energy you can't have."

"Is she talking about love?" Usha thought, "Nah. That has no power."

"You probably don't understand. You can't understand. Usha, you need to die for your crimes. You have murdered many and you tried to murder Skye."

"Why is she referring to herself in the third person? I think I'm going to leave now..."

Usha took a step back as Skye's body took the staff and pointed it at her. Usha screamed and ran into the nearby jungle to get away from the strange and possessed Skye.

"What the hell was that?" Usha pondered, "She was possessed by something. That Demon thing inside of her said I needed to die for my crimes, but it was committing a crime of nature by controlling her body! Whatever. I'll just kill that... tattoo... too!"

Usha's next target was Volf. He was walking along the beach by himself. He went to an area hidden behind some rocks which the group used as a toilet of sorts.

As Volf walked into the hidden area, Usha was already inside and waiting for him. Volf sat down on a rock and did nothing.

"He must just want to be alone..." Usha thought, "Too bad that'll be why he dies."

Usha jumped out from behind a nearby rock and startled Volf.

"Universal Chaos!" he shouted as a powerful and sharp wind chopped her arms and legs off and she flew backward against the rocky wall.

"Dang it!" she shouted, "You broke my back! Now I can't regenerate until it's nighttime!"

"I'll just be stealing this." He said as he took her earring, which was the final piece of the Orb of Night.

"Give that back!" Usha pleaded, "That's the only piece of my outfit that stays intact every time you guys blow me up!"

"No thanks." Volf said as he ran out of the secret area.

"This sucks..." Usha said, "Good thing I can't feel the pain now that he broke my back..."

She waited there until nightfall and her arms and legs began to slither to her across the ground like snakes. Any other chunks of her gathered into a pile and did the same. Everything was reattached. Usha's back then regenerated and she was able to move and feel once again.

"Now I only have early tomorrow to kill them before that ship gets here." She contemplated, "I'm going to be the one to kill them... I'll just kill them tonight! They can't kill me, anyway."

Usha ran to the group's campsite to see Hideaki holding a strange staff.

"What is that staff for?" she studied, "Maybe it has to do with those nine things he's holding that look like my earrings... that they probably stole, too. Whatever, I'm killing them and getting my earring back!"

Usha rose out from inside of a hollow tree trunk and dashed at the group.

"It's Usha!" Skye yelled, "Hurry!"

"You can't do anything, even if you do hurry!" Usha shouted.

"I can do something." Hideaki said calmly, "I just wish we'd done this earlier when Volf got back."

"What are you talking about?" Usha said, "You're holding a bunch of earrings and a stick! What are you going to do – beat me with your cane while doing a tribal dance involving earrings? Is that what those dumb natives here taught you?!"

Hideaki touched final piece of the Orb of Night in Volf's hand and all of the nine pieces merged together into a circular object.

"These aren't earrings."

Hideaki then touched the object with the staff and the Orb and Staff combined.

The circular object on top began to spin, making the flat, circular object look like an orb – the Orb of Night.

Hideaki put the staff straight in front of him and spun himself around counter-clockwise once, clockwise once and counter-clockwise once more. Each time he spun, a beam of energy began to shoot out of another side of the Orb – three in total.

"Aether Trinity of One!" Hideaki shouted at the end of this odd dance.

The three waves of bluish energy combined in front of the Orb of Night into a sphere. This globe of energy then shot at Usha and surrounded her. It spiraled around her for a few seconds and then gathered into a sphere again – this time just above her head.

The ball of energy shot down like a meteorite onto Usha and began to melt.

"It feels like I'm boiling in oil!" Usha shouted, "Help me Obayifo, please!

"You brought this on yourself, Usha!" Obayifo said, "I could have killed them all if you hadn't sent me back!"

"Will you three help me?! Please! I'm begging you!"

"We can't anymore, Usha!" Skye shouted, "It's too late!"

"I'll get you girl!" Usha threatened, "And your little tattoo... too!"

Usha melted to the ground and the only thing left of her was a puddle of bluish Aether energy that quickly washed away in the waves of the ocean upon the sand.

"It's finished." Hideaki said, "Now, at least you two have seen the power the Orb of Night wields."

"Remember what you told us, though." Skye warned, "Using it too much will cause bad problems in the world."

"I know, Skye." Hideaki said, "Believe me, I'm not going to use it too much."

"Anyway," Volf said, "I can't remember, but that last thing she said sounded familiar..."

"Yeah." Skye said, "It was from a musical that traveling circus brought to town a couple months before Leyb attacked."

"Oh yeah!" Volf said, "It was called—"

"It's Sutton's ship!" Hideaki interrupted, "A boat is approaching to pick us up."

"Weren't they coming tomorrow?" Skye asked, "Why are they here tonight?"

"Maybe they saw the bright light and knew that we were awake." Volf said.

"Wow." Skye said, "You actually thought analytically. I'm surprised."

"See, Skye. I'm an analytical thinker. I'm smart."

"No, you're still an idiot. You just got lucky."

"Whatever..."

"Hey, Hideaki!" the first mate said, "Sutton's waiting for you on the ship!"

The group walked through the shallows and hopped into the boat.

Taken to the ship, they thought their troubles were over. Climbing aboard however, they saw something they never could have imagined.

"Hello, Hideaki." Sutton said.

"Sutton! You've become a Vampire!"

"How could you tell?"

"I can tell after looking at Usha for so long. You have black pupils in your eyes - they are pupils, but unnatural pupils nonetheless. Why have you done this, Sutton?"

"I decided that when I lost my Enlightenment that there was no way to be immortal again, so I just accepted it. However, when Usha found me we attacked her and it looked to me that she was dead. Strangely though, when she came walking into the tavern that night she was perfectly well. There was not a scratch on her; that's when I asked if she was an Enlightened or an Old One, since Enlightened can't be ripped to pieces like that. She told me about Vampires: immortal beings just like the Enlightened. I wanted to be immortal again and the Vampire code forces her to turn me into a Vampire if I ask for it. She absorbed my Soul energy – all of it. I thought I was dead, but she gave me back the Soul energy and I was living again, but I was different. I became immortal again, but I was also dead at the same time. I felt like I should be dead, but I had a drive to live. Now, I am forced to kill you by the Vampire code."

"Why must you kill me, Sutton?" Hideaki asked, "Don't you have a will of your own?"

"Vampire code states that we have to kill all Enlightened and anyone we've ever fought. I battled you once a long time ago, before I changed my ways."

"Yes, I remember fighting you at Enclave Trove to defend my personal fortunes hidden there."

"How did you not lose your immortality if you fought him, Hideaki?" Skye asked.

"Loopholes..." Hideaki said.

"I thought you told Yoichi that you didn't know about those..."

"Well... You know – you forget small things every day in short lives, but in a life like this... I forget even the most important of things."

"Anyway," Sutton interrupted, "I have to kill you but I don't have to make it gruesome. Let me kill you with a new weapon from the Northern Poles. It's called a gun."

"Please friend, you've had a long enough life. You don't have to live a life based on death. You're only alive because you steal the Soul energy of others."

"Hideaki, you don't know what being a Vampire is like. I have to kill you. It's not a choice anymore. It's only a choice of how!"

"Then I'm sorry, my friend. Universal Chaos!"

A tornado shot from Hideaki and just barely missed Sutton as it went forward.

"You don't think you can get me with that old attack, do you? I know your fighting styles!"

Hideaki held his staff high and looked up to the sky.

"Penalty of Aether!" Hideaki shouted.

Skies lit up and black clouds encircled the entire Central region of the world. Seas of the world became unstable and waves came crashing down upon the ship and the continents of the world.

Lightning shot through the clouds and gathered in the center position above Hideaki. It then struck the Orb of Night and the energy began to unpredictably hit random things on the ship.

Hideaki pointed the staff at Sutton.

"I am sorry, Sutton."

All storms in the skies almost instantly came down and surrounded the ship. Lightning storms began to strike at Sutton.

"I can't... dodge it..." Sutton muttered incoherently.

Sutton began to melt at many points on his body. Each lightning strike caused a chain reaction starting a new melting point on him.

Finally all that was left of him too was a pool of Aether energy on the ship's deck. Not respecting a vampire, the Aether energies caused rain that washed away any of his remains into the ocean, where he would never be seen again or remembered.

"Goodbye, Sutton." Hideaki said.

The ship continued on through the relentless storms as they tried to reach the border between the border between the Central Jungles and the Eastern Region.

"We're almost there, Hideaki." The first mate said, "I'm very thankful for that. He was a great captain for a long time, but his time came and went. He should have already been dead. We pirates will never forget how you helped us out, Hideaki."

"Don't mention it…" Hideaki said, "Seriously, don't mention it at all. It makes me sad to know that I had to kill Sutton."

"Alright, Hideaki. We'll respect that."

"Thank you, captain."

"No, I'm just the first mate…"

"Not anymore."

"Yeah, I guess I am captain now that… that stuff happened."

"Then let's get to the border, captain Grim!"

"You remember my name. I'm glad."

"I'm sure you'll be even gladder after hearing this: even with Sutton dead, you will still be needing money to keep order in Southern Harbor."

"So, I can have your treasure at Enclave Trove?!"

"If you promise to use it to keep order in Southern Harbor."

"Definitely!"

"Then it's yours!"

"That's awesome, Hideaki. I'll go pick it up with the other guys once we've dropped you off at the border."

Reaching the border, Hideaki, Skye and Volf left the ship and got onto a small boat with captain Grim. They rowed to the shore and the group exited.

"Goodbye, captain Grim. I wish you good travels along your way to Enclave Trove and back to Southern Harbor. It's a long trip and many things could happen."

"Thanks Hideaki. And I know it'll be hard to get the treasure, but it'll be worth it. Goodbye, friends."

Waves calmed and the skies cleared up over the next few hours. The storms were completely dissipated and the only nightmare left in the world was Leyb and his armies.

NORTHERN POLE

ENCLAVE TROVE

Colony of Leyb

WESTERN REGION

CENTRAL JUNGLES

EASTERN REGION

MIDDLE ISLAND

SOUTHERN FLYING ISLANDS

Sphere Zero

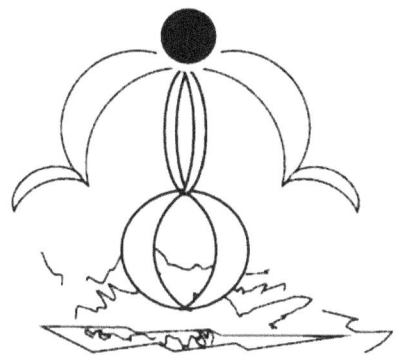

Chapter XIII: Aether, Orb of Night

Ten weeks after their travels began they were right back where they began – the City of Customs. On the other hand, the city was now under the control of Leyb.

Statues of Leyb were scattered about the area and slaves gathered from the Eastern Region and the rest of the world were being forced to constantly build more.

"This place looks terrible." Skye said.

"Yeah." Volf muttered, "I can't even see my home anymore and it's only been ten weeks since we left..."

"The old city is a ruin." Hideaki said, "Anything that was here is now gone and rebuilt in Leyb's image. Take this to heart, you two. Nothing could stop this deranged psychopath from razing the entire region we don't stop him today."

"You're a bit of a speaker, Hideaki." Skye said, "It's annoying."

"Right... Let's just get going, you two."

"Wait. What are you going to do to Leyb, anyway?" Volf asked.

"Use the Orb of Night's special power that I used on Usha."

"But what about the armies?" Skye asked.

"Well... The attack is different than you think. It scales its power based on your target."

"So it could become big enough to stop the entire army?" Volf asked.

"Well... No." Hideaki said.

"Then what are you going to do with it?"

"We're going to sneak into Leyb's new city and find him. Then I'll use the staff against him and his guards. After that we'll escape if we can; if not, then we'll at least have stopped Leyb for good."

"Hopefully it'll work." Skye said, "My family might hate me, but I don't want them to get killed because we couldn't stop Leyb..."

"Nothing will be your fault if we fail, Skye." Hideaki assured her, "Plus, is your father not still an Enlightened? He could stop them if they were to attack, anyway."

"He'd give up his immortality to save our village... But he's so old. I don't think he'll win."

"It's alright, Skye." Hideaki said, "Enlightened don't age in the same way as normal people. We stay healthy and strong for ages."

"You do forget a lot of stuff like all old people, though, Hideaki..." Volf said.

"Idiot..."

"Whatever, Skye. You know it's true."

"Volf," Hideaki whispered, "she's angry because you're making jokes while she's upset."

"Right... Sorry, Skye!"

"It's fine, Volf. I'm ready to go, Hideaki..."

"Very well, Skye. Just remember, your family does love you. I'm sure of it. I know there must be another reason as to why they forced you to leave home."

"Yeah, I guess you're right..." Skye said.

"Where did you live, anyway?" Volf asked.

"In a village all the way on the northern tip of the Eastern Region." Skye said, "I came all the way to the border to leave the region, but I couldn't leave because the border agents wouldn't allow me..."

"Why not?" Volf asked.

"They said I was too weak at first; then after I argued my case they added in another argument. They said that my tattoo looked too suspicious."

"We can't talk anymore, you two." Hideaki said, "We need to stop Leyb. Let's sneak around the buildings to get in."

"Or we could go through the sewers." Volf suggested.

"Gross…" Skye said.

"Back the same way we escaped."

"I guess…"

"Good idea, Volf!" Hideaki praised.

"Cool." Volf said, "I'll lead you to the sewers and you can lead from there."

Volf did as he promised, leading them to the sewers. Hideaki took over and they walked throughout the sewers for hours.

Finding many sealed exits in most places, they ended up coming to the end.

"What's that up ahead?" Skye asked.

"It's my resistance!" Hideaki shouted, "They survived."

Hideaki ran forward with Volf and Skye close behind.

"Who's there?!" a man shouted.

"It's your leader, Hideaki! Two of my followers are with me."

"Everyone!" the man shouted, "Hideaki's back! Leyb didn't kill him after all!"

Flood gates that were blocking the group's way were opened and the group walked inside with the gates closing behind them.

"Hideaki," the man said, "how did you survive?"

"I had the help of these two. They're both unique and powerful in many ways."

"It's great to have you two on the team, then." The man said, "I'm Osei. What are your names?"

"My name's Skye, sir. It's nice to meet one of Hideaki's friends."

"I'm Volf."

"Idiot." Skye said, "Is that all you can do to greet anyone?"

"Sorry, Skye..."

"Never mind... It's fine."

"Wonderful... fighters." Osei said, "Now, let's assemble everyone!"

Everyone left in the resistance and those that had joined the resistance gathered near the center of this large room filled with grates to the surface.

"Hideaki," Osei said, "what's the plan to stop Leyb? Or are we just retreating, for now?"

"We are definitely not retreating." Hideaki said, "I have the Orb of Night and we're going to use it to stop Leyb."

"What's the Orb of Night?" a young female resistance fighter asked.

"It's a powerful artifact from tens of thousands of years ago. We can use it to stop Leyb and at least his guard forces in just one small sweep of this staff."

"Hideaki," Skye said, "I just have to ask this... Why can't you just call up a storm to kill the entire army like on Sutton's ship?"

"That power is used to attack a singular enemy relentlessly. It's great for defeating one opponent, but the energy won't allow it to be used against an entire group."

"Rules of energy are stupid..." Skye said.

"I agree." Hideaki said, "But they're there for a reason, I'm sure. The regular attack will have to suffice."

"There's nothing regular about a magic piece of metal spinning on top of a magic stick..." Osei said.

"Right, right." Hideaki said, "But let's assemble, everyone! We're going to charge the city through these grates. You will all need to distract the soldiers while my two followers and I find Leyb and put an end to him!"

Crowds throughout these sewers cheered at Hideaki's plan, although everyone was unsure about using any sort of magic.

Most people did not believe in Energies, or if they did they did not understand it very well.

"When do we start the attack, Hideaki?" Osei asked.

"Tonight."

"Right, it'll be better to attack when most of the guards are asleep."

Waiting until night fell, the fighters occupied themselves with training. Skye and Volf trained with Hideaki and the fighters began to gather around them to see their amazing Cosmic energies in action.

Finally as the darkness consumed the light of day, the groups assembled at the exits to assault the streets.

"I don't know whether we will succeed or fail." Hideaki said to everyone, "I do, however know that we can't sit here while Leyb and his armies kill our people and demolish our cities and villages. Tonight, we will stop this invasion and put an end to this worst plague ever known to our world – the Lion of the West: Leyb!"

At the sound of this tyrant's name, the resistance fighters poured out into the streets and began to torch Leyb's statues and kill his patrols.

"Come on, you two!" Hideaki shouted.

Volf and Skye followed Hideaki through the city.

"Volf," Hideaki said, "do you know any shortcuts or ways to the capital building? I'm sure that's where Leyb's hiding."

"Yeah," Volf said, "I'll take the lead."

Taking shortcuts through alleyways, pipes, roofs and secret passages led the group to the capital building in only moments.

The capital building was a tall building made of marble; golden statues of Leyb were erected all over this building that used to serve as the house of customs for anyone entering or leaving the Eastern Region.

"I can't see any of our guys out there, yet."

"Don't worry, Volf." Hideaki said, "The resistance is there to distract the soldiers while I use the Orb of Night to destroy the capital building. Any of Leyb's soldiers will have by now gone to fight the resistance, I'm sure."

"You don't think any would stay behind to protect Leyb?" Skye asked.

"Only his generals serve as his guards." Hideaki said.

"Doesn't that mean he only has one guard?"

"Yes, Volf." Hideaki said, "It's also his weakest general: Ornias. He killed only three people before, but he always killed them in ways that would torture the person for days before they could finally die…"

"He doesn't have days." Skye said, "Use the staff, Hideaki."

"Right."

Hideaki lifted the staff in front of him and spun himself around counter-clockwise once, clockwise once and counter-clockwise once more. Each time he went around, a ray of energy shot out from another side of the Orb.

"Aether Trinity of One!" Hideaki yelled.

The three waves of bluish energy combined in front of the Orb of Night into a sphere.

The ball of energy began to pulse and pulled the staff out of Hideaki's hands.

Pulsations of this energy began to push the pieces of the Orb of Night away from one another and finally it imploded.

Imploding the Orb into a small ball, the Aether energy became very concentrated and finally exploded and the pieces flew all around the area.

The pulsating sphere of energy became nine separate pieces and they were absorbed into the nine pieces of the Orb of Night.

Growing with the power of the energy, the pieces became the size of blades to many different swords and knives.

Finally, the nine different pieces came together and formed a strange creature made of blades.

"Aether, Orb of Night…" Hideaki said, "Back into the pipes! Before it sees us…"

The group crawled into the pipes and as they did, the strange creature turned and saw nothing. It looked down at its hands which were two blades.

"I am alive…" it said to itself, "I thought I died. It seems that I will never escape these hateful creatures. If I can't die, then I will finish killing everyone else and be alone."

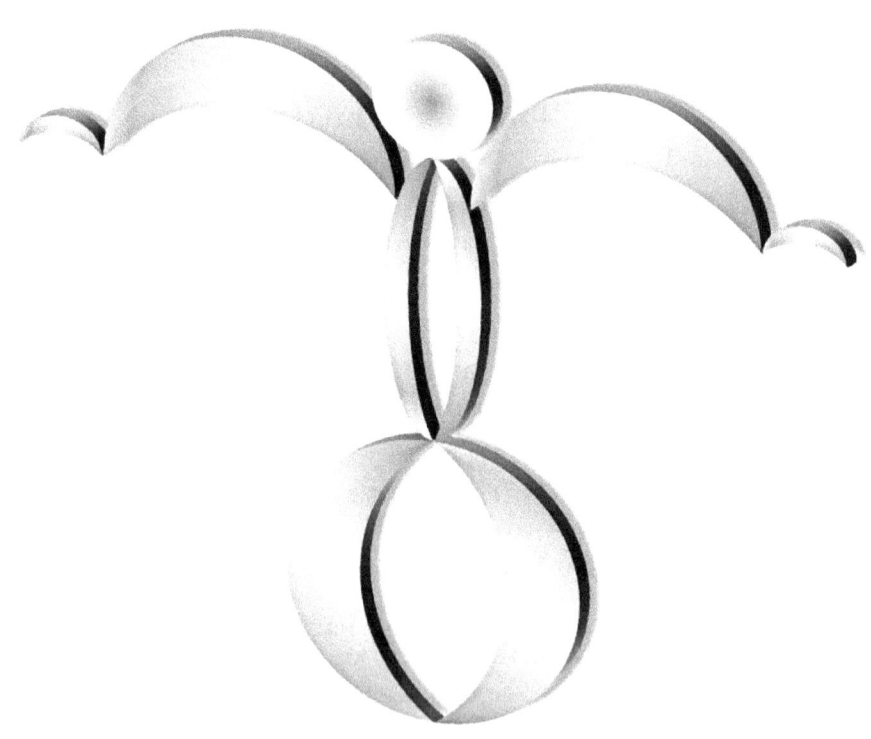

"What is that thing?!" Skye yelled.

"It's the thing I warned you two about..."

"The thing that destroyed the entire Central Region?!" Volf asked.

"Yes," Hideaki said, "I'm sorry, I didn't think that I used it enough times to summon it."

"How many times did you think you had to use it?" Skye asked.

"It was supposed to be three..."

"You did use it three times, Hideaki!"

"Volf's right." Skye said, "You used it against Usha, Sutton and now Leyb!"

"I just thought that only the Aether Trinity of One power being used three times could summon him. I never knew that using any of his powers was enough. Now it will kill so many people... I am so sorry, you two."

"Don't say sorry to us, Hideaki!" Skye yelled, "We have to get the resistance out of here before they all die!"

"There's no time!" Hideaki said, "We will escape with whoever we find on our way back to the sewers and that's all."

"Now you're just being selfish, Hideaki!" Skye said, "You can't even be decent enough to help these people? They're your responsibility!"

"I know, Skye! It's just that I'm the only one that knows how to stop Aether, now. We have to take its staff and destroy it."

"And that will separate the pieces, again?"

"Yes, Skye."

"Then let's go." Skye said, "We have no choice but to run, I guess. I wish we had just attacked Leyb in a regular way... Then we'd at least have a chance right now."

While the three of them attempted to escape, Leyb and General Ornias ran into Aether in his rampage.

"What is that thing, Leyb?" Ornias asked.

"I have no idea, you fool. Just kill it!"

Ornias equipped his multiuse spear; this spear had a sharp part at the end like a knife, many spikes on the sides and a hook to grab enemy weapons.

Aether launched its arms and hands at Ornias; Ornias simply slashed at them with his spear and they flew back at the creature.

"I don't remember you being this strong, Ornias."

"Well, sir." Ornias said, "Nazar enchanted my spear and myself before he went off and... well, died."

"Ah, so you're strong, now. But can you use some of his powers with that, as well?"

"Oh, yeah I can!"

"Then freeze that stupid thing so we can escape, you fool!"

"Right, sir! You get your daughter while I hold it off and you come back and we'll go."

"Who cares about her?! I'm escaping with my life, and if you want to escape with yours, I suggest you use that power now!"

"Alright sir!" Ornias said with a cynical laugh, "Frozen Death!"

Ice gathered around the end of Ornias' spear and shot at Aether; the monster tried to block it but it was very effective and froze the creature.

"Good, let's get out of here." Leyb said, "The resistance destroyed half of my colony and this... thing destroyed the other half."

Leyb and Ornias quickly ran north from the city and escaped on foot into the Central Jungles.

Aether, Orb of Night quickly escaped from its frozen state and went on a killing rampage.

"What is that, Evesmerelda?!"

"It's alright, Anastasia." She said, "I'm sure your daddy's coming for us."

"You know my dad doesn't care!" Anastasia said with tears running down her face.

"It's still fine, Anastasia. I'll protect you. Nothing will ever happen to you while I'm around; let's just stay quiet. I don't think it sees us in these pipes..."

Osei and a few of the resistance fighters promptly ran into Aether. They wondered at first what it was as it stared at them, but they soon realized that it was hostile when it began to throw its blades at them.

Fighters fell against this creature with almost no challenge from them whatsoever.

Osei was holding it back for a few moments, but to no avail; Aether surrounded him and sent all of its nine blades into his body – ripping him to shreds.

Aether killed anyone else it came across and began to summon its mighty powers.

"Trinity of One!" it said over and over as blue spheres of energy formed and crashed into the buildings.

The City of Customs was burning and Aether continued to carpet bomb the city with its unique blasts of Energy.

"Who's that?" Skye asked.

"Where?"

"Right there, Volf!" Skye said, "In the pipes up ahead."

"It's a little girl!" Volf said, "And some woman."

"Are you two alright?" Hideaki asked, "We need to leave the city before Aether kills us!"

"We can't go anywhere with you!" the woman said.

"Why not?" Hideaki asked, "I know who you two are. Leyb's daughter and her personal guard. Leyb already fled, no doubt. Aether began his attack near his palace."

"I told you, Evesmerelda!" Anastasia said, "He doesn't care! Let's go with these people."

"But Anastasia, we–"

"We have no choice, Evesmerelda!"

"Fine, we'll go with you guys. You'd better not harm her!"

"If we wanted to harm her, we would have just left you two here!" Skye said.

"We can trust them, Evesmerelda."

"Right, Anastasia..."

Volf led the group through the correct path back to the sewers and the five of them escaped downward.

Aether saw them go into the sewers and rushed downward to attack them.

"Oh no you don't!" Hideaki shouted, "Icy Grave!"

Water from all throughout the sewers gathered and flooded the city in almost an instant.

Collecting into a thick sphere that covered the entire city, the water turned to ice and became invulnerable to even Aether's attacks.

"Trinity of One!" it yelled over and over, but the blasts could not even scratch the powerful shield.

Down in the sewers, the group thought about what to do next. A few of the resistance fighters survived the fight and so did a few prisoners of war from Leyb's army.

"We can't stay here for long, Hideaki." Evesmerelda said, "I'm not going to let that thing hurt Anastasia, whatever it is..."

"It's the Orb of Night." Skye said, "It was a very powerful artifact from thousands of years ago—"

"Then it turned into a monster and tried to kill everyone!" Volf interrupted.

"Where did it come from in the first place?!" Evesmerelda asked.

"We'll explain later." Hideaki said, "Let's leave now, before Aether finds a way through that shield."

"Penalty!" Aether said as storms gathered in the skies.

Lightning began to strike at the icy shield without pause. The shield began to crack and fall down onto the city below. Aether laughed at this effect.

"They will all be dead, soon." It said, "They deserve it for what they do."

Reigning upon the icy shell, the lightning finally began to heat it and make it melt.

Eventually, the shield's energies evaporated and gave way – the ice turned to water instantly and sent water throughout the area – destroying the city and flooding the sewers.

"We made it just in time!" Skye said.

"Yeah, the water's shooting out from the sewer exit, now..." Volf continued.

Water flooded the cliffs around Hideaki's secret base, but the base was unaffected because it was at a far higher altitude.

"We'll retreat to my base." Hideaki said, "We have nowhere else to go now. Aether will find anything that's out in the open."

Migrating to their new home, the people grew angrier at Hideaki because they all knew by then that he was responsible for Aether's revival.

Aether left the City of Customs and headed east; it was ready to kill more people – thinking it had already killed everyone from the City of Customs.

Leyb and General Ornias fled to the west; they were going to retreat back to Leyb's home city in the Western Region.

"You'd better protect me well, Ornias."

"Yeah, I know emperor. But with just the both of us, it'll be hard..."

"Nazar's enchantments better hold up, then!"

"Yes, sir. I'm sure they will."

"Good, then I no longer wish to speak to you."

"What? Are we going to walk in silence the entire way home?"

"No." Leyb said, "We're going to run in silence. Come on!"

"Run? I can't run that far!"

"Then I suppose you'll be left behind and I'll have to brand you as a traitor and have my armies hunt you down."

"Right... I'm sure Nazar's enchantments will allow me to run more than I used to..."

Hideaki and his followers spread the word throughout the region about Aether; armies rose and fell against this monstrosity.

Without a leader, Southern Harbor fell and many nations without armies ceased to exist.

Remnants of Leyb's armies were killed quickly and no trace of his invasion was left in the Eastern Region.

"What are we going to do, Hideaki?" Skye asked, "We don't have any other ancient magical artifacts we can gather to defeat Aether, do we?"

"No, Skye. We don't."

"Then what can we do old man?!" Evesmerelda asked.

"I don't know!" he yelled, "I'm sorry. I just don't know..."

"Then think of something."
Evesmerelda warned, "We all blame you for
this monster's attack."

"It's okay, Evesmerelda." Anastasia
said, "He already told us that he was just
trying to stop my dad. You and I both know
that means he's not a bad person. He didn't
mean for this to happen."

"Right. Sorry, Hideaki. Men just
sometimes get me angry."

"It's fine, Evesmerelda. I blame myself
as well…"

As the first week of Aether's invasion
came within reach, millions of people had
already vanished from the region and went
onto their next life.

Merciless, this ruler of death was
dedicated to wiping out anything in the world
of Sphere Zero.

PREVIEW of the Sequel

Orb of Night:

Ruler of Death

Orb of Night: Ruler of Death

PREVIEW

Fifty thousand years of peace in the eastern region ended in a bloody war with an oppressive western nation.

At the end of the war, Leyb, the vile emperor of the western nation fled back west with his only general left alive.

Out of selfishness, the emperor left his only daughter behind at the mercy of a monstrosity: the Orb of Night.

When Leyb invaded, a man named Hideaki gathered followers and went to find an ancient weapon called the Orb of Night. Unfortunately, the weapon was a dormant monster named Aether.

Now they have to stop this creature before it rampages across the entire eastern region and murders anyone still left alive after the war.

Characters

Name	Description
Leyb	Leyb is the emperor of the most powerful Western nation. He is an oppressive and disgusting man who enjoys killing, torture and destruction. He barely even notices his own daughter and when he does he simply is checking to make sure that she is still ignorant of his wars against the world.
Hideaki	Hideaki is a powerful Enlightened. Giving up his immortality to save his region from Leyb's armies, he is highly respected among most people. Universal Chaos and Body Undoing are his Cosmic energy powers. He is sixty-two thousand three-hundred and eight years old.
Anastasia	Anastasia is Leyb's daughter; she supposedly knew nothing about his wars – but she secretly knew everything. Her personal guard, Evesmerelda told her all she needed to hear. Anastasia's own brother is dead because of her father and now she is looking to take her father out of power as soon as she possibly can.
General Nazar	A mass murderer who killed millions of people in his past using his strange powers through his past Enlightenment. It looked to be that he had power over ice, but it was simply power over time. He froze time, including his immortality from when he was Enlightened, but the Pillar of Fire started his time again and he disintegrated in the consuming fires of time... and the Pillar of Fire didn't help much either.
General Ornias	A disgusting man that murdered three people in terrible ways – torturing them the whole time they were being killed by him.

General Usha	Usha was once found by Leyb, hunting his daughter Anastasia and he gave her an offer. General Usha joined Leyb only for his army that it would bring her and agreed to not kill Anastasia. She was considered an evil goddess of sorts back in her homeland of the Central Jungles. She hunted and killed children for their Souls because she is a Vampire. Usha hunts for Soul power to regenerate her energies and to someday summon her master – Obayifo, the original Vampire who is also an Old One.
Amaya	Hideaki's powerful mother. She has power over water and weather; she is very ancient, but she looks as young as Skye. She is only a little older than Hideaki.
Skye	Skye is a young woman with a terrible power hidden within her tattoo on her forehead; a power that could destroy everything if used incorrectly.
Volf	Volf is a young man that saved Skye's life when Leyb's invasion on the Eastern Region began. He was able to learn one of Hideaki attacks, but it is considerably weaker than Hideaki's version of it.
General Kione	He is married to Ayé. They are said to be only married because they like to cause anarchy in cities by becoming part of their governments in hostile takeovers and then just abandoning the city, leaving the people without law enforcement. However, they really do love each other; they are troubled and disturbing people, though…
General Ayé	She is married to Kione. Becoming a general to Leyb was an easy choice; she got an army, she got to stay with Kione and she still got to do what she loved… and joining Leyb being her only choice to survive against Leyb seemed to be a pretty good reason, too.
Evesmerelda	Evesmerelda is the personal guard of Anastasia, Leyb's daughter. She is a strong and powerful woman who could easily kill anyone that gets in her path, but Anastasia asks that Evesmerelda doesn't kill anyone that she doesn't absolutely have to and that has changed Evesmerelda's attitude over the years. Leyb hired Evesmerelda in the same way that he hired his generals – at a prison in a country that he was invading.

Evesmerelda was in prison for the kidnapping, torturing and murdering of hundreds of men. She was once a campaigner for women's rights in her country, but she went too far and began to murder in vengeance when she knew that never in her lifetime would Evesmerelda see the rights she and all other women in her country deserved. Fortunately, her time in prison allowed her to rethink her life and her goals and when Leyb hired her he asked her to become a general; however, while he was asking her to join him his daughter, Anastasia was attacked by Usha. Jumping to the rescue wasn't Leyb but Evesmerelda; Anastasia was only four at this time and she has told her father and Evesmerelda that she doesn't remember being attacked or anything about that time other than meeting her personal guard and best friend, Evesmerelda.

Yoichi | A very powerful Enlightened. He has known Hideaki for thousands of years and is far older than any known person in the world. Skye and Hideaki think that he is an Old One. Yoichi knows many loopholes through the contract of Enlightenment that allow him to do things in ways that won't take his immortality away.

Sutton | An old pirate leader. He is from Southern Harbor. He usually stays around Southern Harbor Tavern when in town, but he is known to travel the seas for years at a time. He is two-thousand years old; he is an Enlightened.

Yoko | She was once an Enlightened, but she was immortalized inside of a Key by her own choice. She is now a permanent Enlightened – unable to change her path, ever.

Captain Grim | Once the first mate of Sutton's ship, he became the captain after Sutton's very timely death.

Osei | Osei is one of Hideaki's most loyal followers in his resistance against Leyb; he is also one of the first few people that signed up to help in the resistance. Staying in the City of Customs until Hideaki returned, his loyalty never wavered in the face of any sort of danger.

Aether, Orb of Night | The Orb of Night has come to life and seems to be an evil monstrosity; this ruler of death wishes to kill everyone.

Cosmic Energies

Power	Description
Universal Complete Annihilation	This is the most powerful of all known powers in the universe. It has the power to completely annihilate the entire universe or it can be simply used to kill one target. The only known way to survive it is by being either a Vampire or an Enlightened.
Universal Chaos	This power sends literally sharp winds at an enemy. It is a sort of horizontal tornado, but with winds capable of slicing targets to pieces.
Moon's Gravity	Amaya's regular Cosmic power. She uses it to bend other things to her will using the gravity of the moon.
Thunderstorm Shock Therapy	Amaya's very powerful attack. It sends a volley of powerful lightning strikes at any enemy in the area; she could use it to even take out all of Leyb's armies at once if she wanted to.
Phoenix Renewal	Yoichi's seemingly most powerful attack; it summons up a phoenix that can send powerful Cosmic fireballs at enemies and it can even fly him around and to the top of the Southern Flying Islands.
Universal Phoenix	Combining Universal Chaos and Phoenix Renewal created the Universal Phoenix Cosmic power. This summoned up a pillar of fire that reached as high as the sky. It could melt almost anything in the area and seemed to never burn out.
Icy Grave	Creates an almost impenetrable shield around the user. It was used by Nazar against the Pillar of Fire, but failed against its awesome heat.

Frozen Death	Sends a ball of ice at an enemy, freezing them within. Used by Nazar against Yoichi.
Love's Warmth	Sends a blast of heat at the target. This is a special power of Skye's when she utilizes her tattoo's power.
Help me Dark Saint	This opens a portal to another planet that a Vampire is on. This power is used by Usha to summon Obayifo to Sphere Zero.
Planet Crumbler	This Cosmic energy has the power to destroy an entire planet by being shot into a planet's core and destabilizing it. It could also be concentrated at a much smaller level and not harm a thing. Hideaki used it to create light in a dark area.
Universal Crumbler	This Cosmic energy has the power to destroy the entire universe – albeit slowly. It could easily be stopped by the power of a Universal Complete Annihilation attack anywhere on its surface.
Aether Trinity of One	This power is only at one-third of its strength. Its full power can only be reached once more pieces of the Orb of Night have been collected. Another name for this is Trinity of One.
Penalty of Aether	Causes the weather of the world to attack whatever the target is, relentlessly. Another name for this is Penalty.

Terms

Term	Description
Enlightened	Enlightened are immortal beings; they get their powers by strictly following the ways of the Old Ones.
Vampire	Vampires are immortal beings; they get their powers by following the exact opposite of the ways of the Old Ones. Another name for the Vampire is the Dark Saint. They have a terrible Vampire code forcing them to kill many different people for no good reasons at all.
Old One	Old Ones are the most ancient of creatures in the universe; their true species name is the Flyspeck, but they are simply referred to as Old Ones because their true name is lost to history of anyone after the Old Ones.
Dark Saint	Dark saints are immortal beings; they get their powers by following the exact opposite of the ways of the Old Ones. Another name for the Dark Saint is Vampire.
Immortal	A vampire or Enlightened. Being one of these two is the only way to be immortal – at least according to the Old Ones. There are few ways to kill an Immortal being. One: Destroy the planet the immortal lives on. Two: Use Aether energy – the power of the Orb of Night. Three: Be the Ruler of Death.
Shangrat-Lantis	A lost city that was destroyed in a terrible war long ago. It was in the once large Central Region that is now mostly gone. The only remnants of the Central Region are the Central Jungles and Middle Island.

www.ingramcontent.com/pod-product-compliance
Lightning Source LLC
Chambersburg PA
CBHW070917130626

46555CB00001B/171